Dear Reader,

I'm basically a simple, straightforward kind of
guy and I take a simple, straightforward approach
to problems. Like revenge, for example. The
way to even the score with a man who cheated
me seemed obvious: First, destroy his business.
Second, take his woman.

The business part was easy.

I found out right away that the lady was going
to be the problem.

Selena is passionate, warm and sexy as hell.
She's also got a mind of her own and apparently
she doesn't like being used as part of my plan.

But why the heck did she have to run off to
Utah? If she thinks the snow is going to cool
me down, she's got a lot to learn. I didn't get
where I am by playing Mr. Nice Guy.

On the other hand, I've never met a woman
quite like Selena....

York Sutherland

STEPHANIE JAMES
To Tame the Hunter

Utah

Published by Silhouette Books New York

America's Publisher of Contemporary Romance

For Don and Gus, who understood and
encouraged and then skipped to Canada.
Love you both and I'll bet you didn't know
these books would be distributed up there, too,
did you? You can't escape.

SILHOUETTE BOOKS
300 East 42nd St., New York, N.Y. 10017

RECYCLED PAPER

TO TAME THE HUNTER

ISBN: 0-373-45194-6

Published Silhouette Books 1983, 1993

All the characters in this book have no existence outside the
imagination of the author and have no relation whatsoever to
anyone bearing the same name or names. They are not even
distantly inspired by any individual known or unknown to the
author, and all incidents are pure invention.

One

Selena Caldwell sipped the cool white wine and narrowed her hazel eyes consideringly at the man who had just handed her the glass.

"It won't do you any good, you know," she chided conversationally. "I'm fully aware of the reason you're showing all this interest in me, and it's hardly a flattering one." She made a swishing, dismissing movement with her free hand, and the tiny gold flecks in her eyes seemed to gleam for a moment. "Now why don't you trot on back to that statuesque redhead you're supposed to be with tonight and leave me alone? I'm neither amused nor likely to be swept off my feet.

But thanks for the wine, anyway. My glass was quite empty. Very sharp of you to notice that from halfway across the room!'' Her lips curved in a faint, taunting smile of challenge.

One very black brow climbed behind the dark frames of York Sutherland's glasses, and his hard-edged mouth lifted in either a subtle acknowledgment of her intuitive guess or else a mockery of it. Selena couldn't be certain which.

"I'm going to crush Richard Anderson, Selena," York warned very gently in that dark-timbred, ebony-velvet voice. It was a voice that carried the authority and arrogant menace of a large jungle cat. It would seldom need to be raised. "You don't strike me as the kind of woman who wants to be on the losing side. Why don't you drop him?"

Selena shook her head in admiration and outright awe. It wasn't every day one encountered this kind of raw, aggressive power, even here in Southern California where cool displays of power were as fashionable and correct as being seen in the right clothes and in the right places.

"I know about the business rivalry going on between you and Richard, Mr. Sutherland," she returned firmly, "but it doesn't involve me in any way. Even if it did," she added quellingly, "a candid observer would have to agree I'm already on the *winning* side. Not that it matters to me one way or the other, of course, but it's obvious that Sutherland, Inc., is the underdog in this particular conflict.''

"Because my firm is smaller than Anderson & Company? That only makes us hungrier, Selena. Hungrier and more determined. Anderson can't handle his company the way his father did. He hasn't got the talent or the brains or the flair. I'm going to—'' York broke off, as if suddenly deciding not to say too much.

Which was just fine with Selena. As far as she was concerned the lean, darkly powerful man in front of her had already said more than enough.

"If you're all that hungry, Mr. Sutherland, I suggest you try some of the lobster canapés over on the buffet table,'' she drawled invitingly. "They're excellent. And I think you'll find it's much safer to nibble on one of them than to try biting off more than you can chew elsewhere. Now, if you'll excuse me ... ?''

Without waiting for a response Selena whirled on one well-shod heel and swept quickly away through the lively throng of elegantly dressed cocktail party guests. She had only one goal and that was to locate Richard Anderson in the laughing, chattering crowd.

But even as the tide of people flowed around her, forming a buffer between herself and the tall, aggressive man she had left standing in the middle of the floor, Selena could feel the intensity of Sutherland's gray-green gaze as it followed her across the room.

Unfortunately she was beginning to know the strength of will behind that intensity. York Sutherland was intent, all right, intent on winning. An interesting psychological type, she told herself with a flash of wry humor.

Selena had encountered him on two or three occasions during the past three weeks and had pegged him very accurately from the first. York Sutherland saw the world in simple terms: winners and losers. He had no doubt in which segment he intended to find himself. The man had all the sharp, savage instincts of a born winner.

He *was* rather fascinating, Selena thought— not for the first time—as she made her way to the side of the room and took up a stance beside a gold brocade backdrop curtain that lined the wall. But it was the sort of deadly fascination one felt for any well-adapted predator, she reminded herself grimly. It was a source of irritation to her that she couldn't seem to shake the growing interest and challenge he aroused.

There was no denying the jaguar quality of the man. York was thirty-seven years old, Selena had been told, and was rapidly bringing his architectural-engineering firm into the limelight. Based here in Pasadena, California, Sutherland, Inc., had begun to land important contracts that took it beyond the borders of the Los Angeles metroplex. His firm was now competing for business up and down the entire West Coast and would, at the current growth rate, soon be national, rather than regional in scope.

Selena felt certain that York Sutherland wouldn't stop until the company had become multinational.

It was the nature of the man to keep widening his territory until some immovable object finally got in the path of the irresistible force he seemed to wield. A true winner. It could only be hoped, Selena told herself firmly, that the immovable object showed up relatively soon for Sutherland's sake. He needed to learn a lesson in the fine art of losing gracefully. Then, again, she decided philosophically, perhaps the winners of this world weren't meant to experience that particular phenomenon.

A little rational humility, a touch of a more relaxed, easygoing attitude toward life's challenges, combined with his basic strengths, would make York Sutherland more than aloofly fascinating. It would make him downright irresistible!

She grimaced at the too-honest realization, covering the wry expression by taking a sip of her wine as she scanned the handsome crowd. The ornate, gilded ballroom was dappled with the glow of crystal chandeliers, and the expensively clad guests mingling below seemed right at home in their surroundings. The gala was being sponsored by a local Pasadena organization devoted to raising funds for the arts. It was inevitable that Richard would bring her and equally inevitable that York Sutherland would somehow arrange to attend. Selena was beginning to have the prickling sensation of danger that comes to any animal when it is being stalked. Yet she'd only met him briefly two or three times....

The man who was beginning to seem like her nemesis was out of sight at the moment. Selena told herself it was Richard for whom she was searching the crowd, but it was the image of a sleek, corporate jaguar that stayed in her mind.

There was nothing overtly handsome about York Sutherland but Selena doubted that fact worried him in the least. It was the sense of growing clout, power, and success that he radiated and chose to emphasize. If he had been in any way anxious or uncertain about his personal looks, he would probably have opted for contact lenses instead of the heavily framed glasses he wore. And the thick, midnight-dark hair would have been styled by a professional hairstylist rather than cut by a traditional, conservative barber.

That heavy pelt of black hair was echoed in the darkness of eyebrows that could intimidate with only a casual arch. Behind the lenses of the glasses, long jet-colored lashes hooded a direct, pinning gray-green glance that gave the impression the man wasn't vulnerable in any way. A survivor.

Rough-hewn features etched the fiercely male landscape of his face. A forceful jaw, assertive blade of a nose, and sharply cut cheekbones left no room for any trace of softness.

There was a sinewy grace in the lean, strong body, a supple coordination that spoke of health and exercise. He was the kind of man, no doubt, who religiously swam every day or who ran a couple of miles without fail every morning. It all made for a hard litheness that lent his clothing an impeccable and unique style. Tonight the close-fitting black evening outfit York wore contrasted dramatically with the crisp whiteness of a formal shirt. All very traditional.

York's intrinsic style would be traditional and conservative, Selena reflected, regardless of what he wore. It only served to make her more aware of him in the flashy, ultramodern Southern California environment. He was a jaguar prowling among peacocks.

There was only one reason such a creature would have singled her out. Selena wasn't under any illusions about that fact. She had been seeing Richard Anderson for almost a month and was well aware of the underlying hostility and rivalry between the two men. The current engineering contract for which both firms were competing was lucrative, but no one needed to tell Selena that the animosity between Sutherland and Anderson had its roots in something deeper than routine business competition.

Like it or not, it appeared that as long as she and Richard continued to date she would be caught up in the sophisticated warfare York Sutherland was waging. He saw her as another means of reaching his goal.

Almost from the first Selena had recognized the fact that York wanted to take her away from Richard Anderson. It was a rather primitive tactic and certainly not very flattering to the woman involved. York didn't want her for herself. He only wanted to score another victory against Richard.

No, she wasn't being stalked because of her devastating beauty. Selena had acknowledged that from the beginning. She was thirty-one years old and had no illusions about having been blessed with such beauty that no man could resist her! Selena smiled to herself at the thought and her inner laughter flared for a moment in her hazel eyes.

Reasonably attractive might be a legitimate description, she thought when she was in a charitable mood toward herself. But she knew only too well how much even that limited accolade owed to a pair of contact lenses, two years spent wearing braces on her teeth in high school, attention to her diet, and a painfully acquired sense of style.

It would have been nice to have acquired a classic bone structure and a few extra inches of height from her forebears, but Selena got along surprisingly well with what she had. The animation of intelligence and humor in her face compensated more than she realized for the lack of perfect features. They combined to attract on a more subtle level than sheer beauty could have done. And there was an added appeal in the faint tilt of the gold-flecked hazel eyes; a suggestion of warmth and laughter that was often reflected in the curve of her mouth.

A shining cap of chestnut brown hair was parted in the middle and cut to frame her face in a simple style that moved with casual ease whenever she turned her head.

Selena had learned to enhance the small hint of drama her dark hair had provided with a taste in clothes that favored strong, rich colors. The gown she wore tonight was a perfect example. It was a silk crepe de Chine done in a rich shade of yellow that contrasted beautifully with the chestnut color of her hair. Ruffled at the deep neckline and long-sleeved, it was a narrow swath of color that fell to her ankles. Small gold evening sandals and delicate touches of gold at throat and ears completed the strong yellow line, a line that was cut with a devastating sweep of royal purple and gold in the shape of a carelessly flung silk shawl. It certainly wasn't the most expensive dress in the ballroom this evening but it was definitely one of the most striking.

The gown flowed lightly over small, tip-tilted breasts, a narrow waist, and rounded hips. With only five feet three inches of height to her credit, keeping the figure in line took some effort. Unlike York Sutherland, Selena didn't bother with the discipline of routine exercise. In general, she simply didn't care for routine and discipline. Life was too full of the interesting and the unexpected.

She was in the process of considering that aspect of her nature when she finally spotted Richard's fair head as the crowd parted for a moment. He caught her eye and smiled across the room, starting toward her. Not an easy task, as his prominence in the community caused several acquaintances to stop him with claims on his attention. This wasn't the first time during the evening that he had been separated from her.

A month ago Selena would have rated her chances of having Richard Anderson as an escort as even more remote than the odds of York Sutherland being genuinely interested in her. But that was before she and the handsome boss of Anderson & Company had been drawn together by a mutual interest.

"I've been looking for you, honey," Richard murmured as he drew close and took her arm. "Come on, let's get out of here for a few minutes. What a crowd!" His vivid blue eyes smiled down at her affectionately.

Richard was close to Sutherland's age, perhaps a year younger. Both men had assumed the reins of architectural-engineering firms at an early age, but there the resemblance stopped.

Where Sutherland was dark and bluntly aggressive, Richard was fair, almost patrician. He had the wealthy background of a well-established Pasadena family behind him, and the good breeding and education showed. There was none of the hard-edged look that marked York. Richard had inherited Anderson & Company from his father, who had died two years earlier. The son had been properly groomed for the position. York had built his own firm from the ground up. Selena was a great deal more comfortable around Richard, in spite of the differences in their backgrounds, than she was around York Sutherland.

"I got ambushed by your business friend," she told her escort dryly as they slipped out of the ballroom and into the ornate lobby of the magnificent old hotel. Perched atop a hill with a commanding view of the San Gabriel Valley, the grand building was a Pasadena landmark.

Richard winced as they moved across the chandelier-lit lobby. "I shouldn't have left you alone. Did he bother you?"

"Not particularly. But what has that man got against you, Richard? Or is he always that way toward competitors?"

"I'm afraid it's his natural approach to any contest. He likes to win," Richard muttered grimly as they stepped outside onto the terrace.

Below, the formal gardens lay in shadowed darkness, but beyond, the gleaming lights of the countless towns and cities that all went under the name of Los Angeles blazed in the night. It was still winter but here in California it seemed more like spring. There was a nip in the air but Selena wasn't uncomfortably cold. A few minutes here on the terrace would be a pleasant change from the warm, crowded ballroom.

"Do you think he's—" she hesitated, searching for the right word, and wound up using the one she meant "—dangerous?"

Richard laughed, slipping an arm around her waist. "Hardly. What can he do? He's probably a bit upset at the moment because he doesn't like the thought of losing another contract to me so soon after Anderson & Company walked off with the last one! It was a project Sutherland thought he should have had. He doesn't always like the idea that his firm is still a lot smaller and that Anderson & Company has been around a lot longer. We're bound to have an edge over him, and now that he's nibbling around at the big time, he's annoyed at the looks of the competition. That's his problem." Richard shrugged with the indifference of the man at the top for those still struggling below.

"I think he's bent on causing trouble, Richard," Selena suggested carefully. She didn't want to imply that trouble might be more than Richard could handle, and for her own pride's sake she didn't want to imply that the trouble promised by York Sutherland might be more than *she* could handle! Richard had the right attitude. What could the other man do, practically speaking? Still, deep down inside in a very hidden, very feminine part of her, she knew York was on the prowl and nothing she could say was going to dampen the flicker of wariness the man had aroused in her during the past couple of weeks.

Those first few meetings with York had been entirely casual, entirely harmless, if judged by concrete evidence. But she had sensed what lay behind the polite, testing remarks. And tonight the kid gloves had come off completely. York had made it clear that he wanted to take her away from Richard Anderson. When he'd found her temporarily alone in the crowd and thrust the glass of wine into her hand, she had known there could no longer be any doubt about his intentions.

"What can he do?" Richard soothed. "I don't think he'll risk anything really outrageous. After all, the man has a business reputation to protect. And if he wants to continue mingling with the sort of people he's with tonight, he'll watch his step!"

"Which brings up the interesting question of what he *is* doing here tonight," Selena observed. "He hardly strikes me as a patron of the arts! I certainly haven't heard his name mentioned as a collector or a major contributor to fund-raising projects like this one!"

Richard laughed. "I'm afraid he's more interested in social climbing than art. He's smart enough to know that being seen at this type of function is a plus for him, though."

And he knew we'd be here, Selena added silently. It was difficult to slap the label of "social climber" on York Sutherland. The term implied a barely concealed desperation and a fawning attitude that simply didn't fit the man. No, she trusted her own intuition too much to accept that simple explanation of his behavior. York had his own reasons for being here this evening and they probably didn't have much to do with social climbing.

Besides, any man truly interested in climbing the social ladder would hardly have wasted so much time cornering her! She was as much an alien in this crowd of wealthy, established people as he was! Well, almost as much of one.

"Don't worry about him, Selena," Richard declared. "If he causes any problems, I'll take care of him."

She heard the easy certainty in his words and wondered at it. Were they talking about the same man? But she had to uphold her end, so she smiled at the good-looking man beside her. "You're right. There's not much he can do, is there?"

"Nope." Richard drew her closer with an inviting expression. "I'm not even going to start worrying if he makes a pass at you!"

"Thanks a lot! A little jealousy is good for a man!" she protested, laughing.

"He's not your type," Richard assured her, bending his head to take her lips. "That much is easy to see."

"Ummm." She let her agreement hover between them as he kissed her, folding her close. After all, it was the truth, wasn't it? York Sutherland wasn't her type at all. Fascination hardly constituted attraction!

It was very pleasant in Richard Anderson's arms. He was an attractive man who was not without a certain finesse in the fine art of romance. Selena took pleasure in his warm embraces although she hadn't yet reached the point of wanting to pursue the romance into a full-fledged love affair.

Not that Richard hadn't attempted to persuade her. She knew he wanted an invitation to her bed; knew, too, that he thought it was only a matter of time. Selena was grateful that he was willing to let her set the pace of the relationship. His understanding and sensitivity were two of the characteristics she appreciated most in him.

"I suppose we should be getting back." Richard sighed, lifting his head reluctantly. "Although with a little provocation I could probably be persuaded to stand out here all night . . . !"

"I wouldn't dream of interfering between you and your duty to the arts," Selena murmured teasingly.

"You could try," he complained good-naturedly, guiding her back toward the lobby.

Selena was about to make a quick, light retort but the words died on her tongue as she saw the slight, shadowy movement at the far end of the terrace. A man had stood there, lost in the protective darkness of the ornamental shrubs. There was no sign of him now but instinct told her it wasn't just any guest who had stepped out onto the terrace. It had been York Sutherland.

Damn the man! What did he hope to accomplish by stalking her this way? She certainly didn't see herself as Richard Anderson's vulnerable point! What kind of meaningless victory would it be to take her away from Richard? The answer came in the next breath. It would be a psychological victory. A small one, perhaps, given Richard's varied social life and the ready availability of other women, but nevertheless a definite coup. Well, she wasn't a pawn to be used. She would take a leaf from Richard's book and treat York Sutherland as if he simply didn't matter very much.

They reentered the glittering ballroom and almost immediately Richard was once again commandeered—this time by an elderly and influential member of the society that was sponsoring the evening's gala.

"If you'll excuse me for a few minutes?" Richard said with wry apology as the matronly woman clutching his arm began to drag him away.

"Of course." Selena smiled benignly. She understood that this evening was as much a business event as a social one for her escort. He had a purpose here tonight and that was to garner contributions. Richard had his duty.

She was actively considering the possibility of another trip to the buffet table and was trying to talk herself out of it when York materialized at her side.

"Will you dance with me, Selena?" he asked calmly as if he fully expected an affirmative answer.

She smiled brilliantly up at him. Such aggression deserved a blunt answer. "No," she replied simply and without any compunction at all.

His hard mouth quirked. "You'll be perfectly safe out on the dance floor."

"You never give up, do you?"

It was his turn to make a blunt reply. "No."

She tilted her head to one side and studied him as if he were an interesting specimen under a magnifying glass. The challenge hung in the air between them, baiting her and angering her. "I'll make a deal with you," she offered softly.

There was a tiny silence while he considered that. "I'm listening," he drawled.

"I'll dance one dance with you if you'll give me the satisfaction of admitting the truth about why you're interested in me," she dared gently.

"Agreed," he said at once, reaching out to take her arm. She felt the heat of his hand as it closed around the yellow silk and she drew in her breath with a small sense of shock. "First the dance . . ." he said coolly.

"Oh, no," she contradicted, not moving. "First the honest explanation."

The long, sable lashes shifted behind the lenses of his glasses, hooding the gray-green eyes as he considered. "I sense an impasse," he growled softly. "Neither one of us is going to trust the other to carry out the terms of the bargain, so neither one of us is going to pay off first."

"Ah, well, it might have been interesting," Selena tossed back easily and tried to disengage her arm from the manacle of his fingers. He didn't let her go.

"It probably would have been," he agreed, starting forward with her arm still firmly in his grasp, "because you didn't intend to carry out your side of it, did you?"

"No," she admitted unhesitatingly. "You're hurting my arm, Mr. Sutherland." His forward momentum was making it difficult to dig in her heels. Doing so would cause a scene and Richard would never forgive her for that, regardless of the circumstances!

"Stop fighting me, Miss Caldwell, and you won't get hurt," he advised dryly as he swept her through the doors and out into the lobby.

"I have the feeling one has to keep fighting you or else one will get trampled!" Selena bit out, infuriated at the ease with which he had swept her out of the ballroom. In another moment they would be through the lobby and back out on the terrace. Still she could see no way of stopping him, short of screaming the hotel down.

"Not true," he objected as he reached the terrace with her in tow and finally came to a halt. "Not true at all," he went on in that velvety voice as he searched her thoroughly annoyed face. "I wouldn't dream of trampling you. There are any number of other things I would rather do... to you... with you...."

Selena shivered suddenly beneath the dangerous gleam that was lighting the near-green eyes. In the shadowy darkness of the terrace York Sutherland's aura of menace was taking on fantastic proportions. She had to get a grip on her nerves!

"I don't believe you, Mr. Sutherland," she got out very bravely, her eyes meeting his unflinchingly. "Don't try to tell me you've been overpowered by my earth-shaking charms! The only reason I've become the subject of your attentions is because you think you can make use of me to get at Richard."

"That's the 'honest reason' you were trying to bargain out of me with the promise of a dance?" He smiled slowly.

"Do you deny it?" she gritted.

"Is it so hard to believe I might want you for, shall we say, more basic reasons?" he countered meaningfully.

"Yes, damn it! I'm not your type and you're not mine. Furthermore—"

"You're Richard Anderson's type, though?" he interrupted deliberately.

"My relationship with Richard is none of your business," she declared with fine hauteur and then spoiled the effect by adding nastily, "For the record, Richard and I met because of a mutual interest and our relationship has evolved naturally out of that foundation. Not because he spotted me on his rival's arm and decided it would be amusing to try to take me away from him!"

"What mutual interest?" York demanded, totally ignoring the rest of her lecture.

She glared at him suspiciously, uncertain about how much to get involved in the absurd discussion but equally uncertain about how to escape it.

"Go ahead," he invited in the small, tense silence. "Tell me about the basis of this profound and solidly based relationship you have with Richard Anderson."

"Art," she finally retorted succinctly, satisfied that he couldn't counter the statement by claiming an equal interest.

"You're an artist?" he pressed.

Selena eyed him calculatingly. "No, I manage a local artists' supply store."

"And Anderson just wandered in one day to buy a paintbrush?"

The mockery in his words goaded her. "Are you enjoying yourself at my expense, Mr. Sutherland?"

"I'm beginning to, yes," he admitted with a flickering smile.

"Then by all means carry on without me!"

For the second time that evening Selena attempted to whirl on one heel and walk away from York Sutherland. This time, however, she didn't get far. He never released his grip on her arm.

"Please wait," he urged in a tone that might have passed as apologetic if it hadn't been in such direct contradiction to the commanding strength of his fingers. "I really would appreciate an answer to my question."

"Why should I bother?" she snapped.

"Because everything about you, including your relationship with Anderson, interests me."

"You mean everything about Richard Anderson interests you and at the moment I happen to be involved with him. Therefore, I interest you."

Selena's hazel eyes sparkled with the force of her annoyance. Yes, that was the right word. She was annoyed with this man, not afraid of him!

"Your logic is impeccable if one accepts the basic premise," York said thoughtfully.

"Are you going to deny the basic premise? That your one goal is to find a way to defeat Richard?" she challenged.

"A man can have more than one goal at any given time," York reminded her calmly.

"You're impossible. Why can't you at least be honest with me?"

"You haven't answered my question," he persisted very quietly.

"About the basis of my relationship with Richard? I see no reason why I should!" She stepped backward abruptly, hoping to take him off guard and, to her astonishment, she succeeded. He released her arm.

"You want a reason?" he mused, watching the small flash of triumph cross her features as she found herself free. "How about if you don't give me the answer I'll follow you back inside, throw you over my shoulder, and carry you out here where I will keep you until you finally decide to talk?"

Selena arched a speculative eyebrow, not fooled by the almost whimsical tone of his voice. A short dash would take her out of his reach, but he could easily catch up with her in the lobby. "Strangely enough I can almost imagine you doing that, even though it would make fools out of both of us in front of everyone!"

He shrugged and said nothing, waiting.

"Does the answer mean so much to you, then?" she prodded wonderingly.

"Yes."

Selena lifted one silk-clad shoulder in an answering shrug. What harm was there in simply telling him the truth? Perhaps if she did he would realize how little chance he stood of interrupting her romance with Richard Anderson.

"All right, I'll tell you." Her lips curved slightly in a fleeting smile. "I don't mind losing such a small battle."

"Small battles make up wars," he warned softly.

"Only in your book. Not all of us see everything as a win-lose proposition," she responded tartly. "The answer to your question is simple. Richard was trying to persuade a local artist to accept a commission for the artwork in the new Anderson & Company building down near South Lake Avenue. Someone told Richard I might have some influence, since I've gotten to know a lot of artists in this area in the course of my work. I acted as a kind of interface between the temperamental painter and the logical business-man. While all the negotiations were going on, Richard and I had an opportunity to discover that we had a great deal in common. We're both heavily involved in the art world and we both have a foot in the business world. There you are. Simple answer for a simple question. We've been dating regularly ever since,'' she concluded in liquid accents.

"I see . . ."

"I'm ever so glad you do, Mr. Sutherland. Having ransomed myself, I'll try saying good-bye. Again."

"Not yet," he murmured, reaching out once more to catch hold of her. This time he had cir-cled her wrist before she'd realized his intention. "There's something else we must discuss . . ."

"You're beginning to try my patience," Se-lena hissed. "And I believe I've spent enough time out here on the terrace tonight!"

"Your first trip out doesn't count." He drew her inexorably closer, apparently fascinated by the anger in her. "You were with the wrong man."

Selena's eyes narrowed sharply at that, her anger metamorphosing into another emotion she didn't want to acknowledge. It might have been fear, judging by the faint trembling that raced along her nerve endings. Or it could have been something else. Excitement? Fascination?

Belatedly she put up her hands, her amethyst and gilt nails splaying across his shoulders in protest. The gray-green gaze locked with her own, blazing with masculine promise.

Selena had only time enough to call herself a fool for having gotten into the situation and then it was too late. His mouth was claiming hers.

Two

Claiming was an all too accurate description, Selena realized, her nails biting deep into the black fabric of his evening jacket. In that moment she could not have said whether the small punishment she managed to inflict was in retaliation for his breathtaking aggression or a means of maintaining her balance beneath the onslaught.

She needn't have worried about falling. His arms wrapped around her, rough palms molding the slender line of her back beneath the yellow silk. Another tremor went through her as he slid his hands down her spine to find the small, sensitive place just above the curve of her hips. And then he was pressing, urging her closer into the heat of his body.

On her lips his mouth moved with heavy sensuality, exploring, staking a claim, threatening to overwhelm. Selena's senses seemed dazed as she automatically tried to adjust and react to the situation. There was none of the pleasant warmth she experienced with Richard's arms, nor did York Sutherland's embrace remind her in any way of the sometimes casual, always frustrating lovemaking she had known with her ex-husband three years ago.

The thought of her ex-husband acted like a slap, bringing her whirling thoughts into sharp focus for an instant. The marriage to Cale Masters had ended in divorce a year and a half after it had begun. It was not a subject she chose to review very often. What had made her think of it now?

She knew the answer to that. She was instinctively making comparisons, relating York Sutherland's assault on her senses to the kind of sensuality to which she had been exposed in her marriage.

But everything she had known with Cale, as well as the light romances she had allowed herself to become involved with since the divorce, faded before the flaming demand she faced to-night.

He was seeking to forge a bond, she realized, striving to overwhelm her defenses and take her captive. Everything would be so much simpler for him if he could manage that.

Selena tried to pull away, tried to shatter the bonds before they could become too strong.

"York! Stop it. You have no right!"

He caught the nape of her neck in his palm, holding her head still as she struggled to break the electric contact. Beneath the curve of her chestnut hair his fingers moved in a soothing, persuasive way, deliberately gentling her as if she were a wild creature he wanted to tame.

"Don't fight me, Selena," he coaxed huskily, his mouth barely grazing her lips. "There's no need . . ."

She heard the thick velvet of his voice and gasped at the audacity of the man. No need! There was every need to fight him! He was dangerous. . . . But his mouth closed once more over hers and this time the warmth of his tongue became an insistent, demanding pressure. Everything was happening much too fast. Her instincts were to give ground and fall back in an effort to regroup her forces.

She made herself stand very still, remotely passive in his grasp, but the seeking, probing pressure on her mouth refused to recognize such tactics. His tongue skated along her lower lip in a seductive, provocative attempt to force an opening. When she refused the admittance, he retaliated by sliding his thumb along the line of her jaw and up to the corner of her mouth where he pressed.

Simultaneously York caught the softness of her lip ever so gently between his teeth and nipped. He never hurt her, Selena realized vaguely, but in every small attack the threat was implicit. He wanted the intimacy of her mouth and was determined to take it.

She told herself she would only give enough to put him off his guard and enable herself to get free. Hesitantly she parted her lips, only to realize immediately that she had made a mistake.

"Selena!"

Her name was a groan of satisfaction and intent. The sound was nearly lost as he took advantage of her small surrender to sweep into the dark recesses of her mouth. Selena shivered as his tongue moved triumphantly through the newly conquered territory, seeking out any last vestige of resistance. Unwilling to give up the fight, she struggled vainly in his arms.

It was an insidious battle because it sparked its own dangerous kind of excitement. The more she fought him, the more violently aware of her own awakening desire she became. Selena saw the trap waiting for her and began to panic.

Hastily she slid her hands up from his shoulders to the strong column of his throat and sank her nails into the vulnerable area beneath his jaw. The effect was immediate.

"What the hell . . . ?"

The affronted maleness in him was palpable. York lifted his head to glare down at his victim, eyes glittering and narrowed. His hands tightened on her as she faced him with all the composure at her command.

"That's enough, Mr. Sutherland! I wish to return to the ballroom. Your primitive approach to the art of lovemaking does not appeal to me in the least!"

"You mean it scares the hell out of you," he countered tightly. Even in the dim light slanting out onto the terrace Selena thought she could detect an angry red stain high on his cheekbones, and there was no doubt at all about the flash of controlled fire behind the lenses of his glasses.

"It *annoys* the hell out of me!"

His hand still gripped her nape as he searched her over-bright eyes. "Believe it or not, annoying you is not my intention," he finally allowed, some of the hardness disappearing from his voice. "I only wanted to make you aware of me..."

"Well, you've certainly accomplished that! Do you always resort to such aggressive tactics when you're engaged in a business competition?" she shot back ironically.

"You think that kiss had something to do with my intention to crush Anderson?" he inquired dryly.

"Why else would you be expending all this energy on me?" Selena charged waspishly.

There was a slight pause during which she assumed he was searching for the words with which to deny the accusation, but when he spoke again, he managed to surprise her.

"Would it be so bad if my interest in you happened to dovetail very neatly with my plans for Anderson & Company?" he finally asked carefully.

Selena stared at him and then raised beseeching eyes to heaven. "My God! I don't believe this! Of course it would be bad! It would be disgusting, abominable, infuriating, and totally reprehensible! Are you out of your head? What you're really asking is if I would mind being *used!* The answer to that is yes, I would mind!''

''Even if we discover in the process that we're made for each other?'' he taunted lightly.

''Impossible,'' she grated. ''If ever two people were *not* made for each other, those two people are you and I.''

''Is that why you were trembling just now in my arms?'' he whispered, the strong hand on her nape moving with hypnotic tenderness down her throat to the ruffled front of the yellow silk gown.

''A woman can tremble from anger as well as passion, Mr. Sutherland.'' Selena held her breath as his touch came to a halt on her delicate collarbone. She was torn between the desire to flee and the need to demonstrate the fact that he couldn't intimidate her. Chin lifted coolly, she held his hooded gaze.

He smiled crookedly. ''And right now nothing on the face of this earth could get you to admit that what you were feeling a moment ago was the beginning of passion and not anger, correct?''

''Perfectly correct.''

''I'm willing to admit that what I felt was desire,'' he drawled softly.

"I congratulate you on your ability to channel your passions so that they serve your business interests!" Selena flared tightly. "But I suppose that's natural for someone like you."

"Someone like me?" he prompted, his smile fading.

"A winner. That's what you are, isn't it, York Sutherland? A man who sees everything in terms of winning and losing. You're determined to make your way to the top and you'll use anyone or anything you can to get there. Your immediate goal is to win out over Anderson & Company, isn't it?"

The harsh contours of his face seemed to harden but he didn't deny the accusation. "I intend to defeat Richard Anderson. Totally."

"Well, I refuse to be used in the process!"

"Especially since you think it's Anderson who will win?" he prodded.

"I'm not choosing sides in the hopes of finding myself on the winning team, Mr. Sutherland. It just so happens I like Richard a great deal more than I like you!"

She stepped backward a small pace, preparing to put a great amount of distance between them. Somehow his fingers, which had been hovering in the ruffle of the dress, slipped down the silk to the tip of one breast. The heat of his hand burned through the material, sending shock waves through her body as her nipple reacted to the touch.

Knowing he must be aware of her body's reaction was enough to hold her paralyzed for an instant longer. Their eyes met for a timeless moment, and in the darkening green depths of York's gaze Selena read the signs of a raw and ravishing hunger.

There was nothing that could be said. Selena could think only in terms of escape and spun away from York's touch and the promise in his eyes, moving blindly across the terrace toward the relative safety of the lobby. An instant later she was temporarily out of reach of the predator in the shadows. Without pausing to glance back, she made her way to the ballroom.

It was a great relief not to catch another glimpse of York Sutherland for the rest of the evening.

By nine o'clock the next morning the image of York as a predatory jaguar was safely buried in the farthest corners of her subconscious. Selena went about her work with her customary enthusiasm, supervising clerks, advising customers, and handling the myriad problems large and small that occurred every day in her busy world.

But while the fantasy was buried, her common sense was not.

In the clear light of a California morning it was easy enough to tell herself she had overreacted to York's stalking presence; still, where there was smoke...

There could be no doubt about the man's intentions, she thought as she checked the supply of acrylic paints and silkscreening materials prior to filling out an order form. Sutherland was out to thoroughly crush Richard. The idea should have been laughable, given her knowledge of the Anderson fortune and Richard's standing in the community. But she couldn't quite bring herself to laugh it off completely, in spite of Richard's failure to take the threat seriously.

Well, the only thing she could do was stay clear of the hunger, she decided resolutely as she straightened from her task and started toward the counter where three clerks were busy handling customers. Richard could handle his own business problems, if he had them. He certainly didn't need her advice! Her only experience in the world of business was managing Artistic Endeavors. Her mouth lifted in a smile of unconscious pride as she glanced around the large artists' supply shop. It wouldn't be long before she would seriously be able to consider owning the place. The Fletchers had talked often about selling in order to be freer to pursue their jet-set lifestyle.

As if thinking of the owners of Artistic Endeavors had triggered a switch somewhere, the phone rang behind the counter and a moment later a clerk called her.

"It's Mr. Fletcher, Selena."

"I'll take it in the office, Alison." She hurried toward the cramped room at the back of the store where she had a small desk and several file cabinets. One of the first things she intended to do after taking over ownership of Artistic Endeavors was to expand that poor excuse of an office. It might serve for a *manager* but a *small business executive* deserved something more sophisticated.

"Good morning, John," she greeted her boss cheerfully. "Calling to tell me you're on your way to Utah?"

"I'm calling to tell you Utah is out, Tahiti is in," John Fletcher announced grandly. "Louise changed her mind last night. We'll be leaving at four o'clock tomorrow afternoon."

"Tahiti! What about your condominium at the ski resort in Utah? I thought you and Louise always went skiing in the winter. It's one of those time-share arrangements, isn't it? If you don't use the two weeks you're scheduled for, you won't be able to get back into the condo until your turn comes up next year."

"Which brings up the reason for this call," John Fletcher retorted with a chuckle. Selena automatically smiled in response. She was fond of John and Louise Fletcher. A middle-aged couple of independent means, they thoroughly enjoyed the good life their money could buy.

Artistic Endeavors had been but one of many flights of fancy the Fletchers had indulged. It would have doubtless been sold two years ago when the novelty of running the business and mingling with the artistic clientele had worn off, except that they had recently hired a new manager for the store.

The new manager had thrown herself into the work with the enthusiastic desperation of a woman recovering from a nasty divorce. Selena had arrived in Pasadena from San Diego, where she had left behind a job in an art gallery and an ex-husband who had succumbed to the wiles of another woman. She had been more than a little grateful for the promise of a new career in a new town, and her hard work had paid off. Within six months Artistic Endeavors had nearly doubled its income.

The problem, of course, was that its owners didn't really need the money. By that time, however, they had realized how much the store was coming to mean to Selena and a bargain was struck. They would continue to hold on to the business until such time as their new manager could afford to buy it from them. With any luck and with the generous salary they provided her, Selena expected to be able to manage the purchase in another few months.

"Okay, I'm listening," she said into the receiver. "What's the reason for the call? Did you want me to organize a bon voyage party down at the docks for you?" She'd done that as a surprise for one of the Fletchers' many trips and they had loved it. Virtually all the store's regular customers had shown up at shipside, and the wide variety of unpredictable artistic talent in the group had made for a unique farewell. Incredibly decorated banners, streamers, and some fairly wild music had dominated the normally sedate Long Beach docks that day.

"Not this time, unfortunately," John sighed wistfully. "We're flying. What I'm calling about is to see if you want to make use of those two weeks at the condo in Utah."

"Me!" Selena gasped, startled. "I don't even ski, John!"

"Mingle with the crowd sipping hot toddies in the lodge and no one will ever know that you didn't spend all day falling down a snow-covered hill!"

"What about the store? I couldn't just leave it!"

"Don't be ridiculous. You have to learn to start acting like an owner someday. What are you going to do after the place is yours? Never take a vacation?" he scoffed. "Besides, you know Alison and the others can manage for a couple of weeks. You're the one who trained them!"

"Fledgling entrepreneurs aren't supposed to indulge themselves in lengthy vacations," Selena pointed out on a note of laughter.

"Only inefficient ones can't afford to do it," John corrected staunchly. "At any rate, this is California, not New England. The work ethic is different out here."

"I know," she conceded lightly. "Playing is as important as working. I really appreciate the offer, John, but you've taken me by surprise. Give me a few hours to think about it, okay? Is there anyone else who might want to go?"

"With you, you mean?" he asked suggestively.

"No! I mean instead of me! Someone who skis, for instance!"

"I'm sure if I stood out in the middle of Colorado Boulevard I could find someone, but it's you who should go," he responded dryly. "Louise says so."

"Now that's a tough argument."

"I know. I'd put her on the phone to convince you but she's out buying a new wardrobe of sundresses to replace all the ski gear she bought last week."

Selena laughed. "Let me think about it, John," she begged. "I'll give you an answer this evening. Are you just going to let the condo go to waste this year if I don't take you up on the offer?"

"Yup."

"Sad thought."

"Not when we started picturing the beaches in Tahiti," he informed her promptly.

"I see your point. Thanks for thinking of me. I promise I'll do my best to talk myself into it. Tell Louise I'll call her later tonight."

"We'll be waiting," John told her cheerfully before hanging up the phone.

Two weeks at a ski resort in Utah. And she didn't even ski! Still, it would be an experience, Selena thought as she slowly replaced the instrument on her end. It was true that Alison and the others could probably manage without her for that length of time. There hadn't been much of an opportunity to take a vacation during the past two years....

On the other hand, it might be a little lonely trapped amongst a bunch of ardent skiers without anyone to share the joys of non-skiing with her. What would Richard say? Would he want to come with her?

She shied from the thought almost at once. If she were to invite Richard he would assume the obvious—that she was inviting him to share a bed as well as a condominium. And who could blame him? But she knew she wasn't yet ready for that step in the relationship. She needed a little more time to decide how deep her feelings went. The memory of her disastrous marriage still hovered at the edge of her thoughts whenever she thought of a commitment to Richard. Why couldn't she feel in his arms what she had sensed awaited her in the embrace of York Sutherland last night?

Instantly she repressed that thought, rising to her feet with an annoyed restlessness. Smoothing the narrow skirt of the blue-and-white striped suit she wore, Selena went determinedly back to work.

She still hadn't made up her mind about whether or not to accept the Fletchers' invitation as she let herself into the sunny third-floor apartment she was renting in the lively South Lake Avenue area of Pasadena. The proximity of the California Institute of Technology, the world-famous Huntington Library and Art Gallery, and the beautiful homes of the nearby Oak Knoll area made for an eclectic, interesting mix. All in all, Selena had often reflected, she had found a pleasant oasis in the sprawling, dynamic L.A. region.

It would mean buying a few warm clothes, she thought as she slipped into a slender, ankle-length, T-shirt dress. The comfortable, figure-hugging knit material was a vivid maroon with a bright, wide hem of electric pink. Selena slid her feet into a pair of sandals and went out into the kitchen to start her dinner.

The ringing of the doorbell came just as she was about to throw the handful of pasta into a kettle of boiling water. It could have been worse, she decided, turning off the heat under the water and heading for the door. Whoever it was could have caught her just *after* she'd gotten the pasta into the water!

"Who is it?" she asked, glancing through the tiny peephole with the automatic cautiousness of a Los Angeles resident.

"York Sutherland," came the gravel-and-velvet reply.

Selena's hand fell away from the doorknob as if the metal were molten. It took a startled heartbeat or two to regain her equilibrium. Forcefully she reminded herself that her imagination had run away with her last night. The man who stood outside her door was only a businessman, not a genuine jungle cat.

"What do you want?" she demanded, not opening the door.

"I have to talk to you, Selena."

"In the middle of dinner!"

"Your gracious hospitality is overwhelming me," he murmured dryly.

"I only dispense gracious hospitality to those who know how to be gracious themselves!"

"Selena, please open the door," he said with deliberate patience. "I must talk to you. What I have to say concerns you deeply."

"I'll bet. Say it, then."

"Damn it! I'm not going to stand here talking through this door. If you're so frightened of me, come on out into the safety of the hall. Or we can go down to the pool and sit in the full view of your neighbors!"

"I am not frightened of you and you know it!" she snapped, goaded into unlocking the door and confronting him with an expression of supreme irritation.

He ignored the look, slipping into the room before she quite realized it. With a frustrated exclamation, Selena closed the door behind him, leaning back against it with both hands behind her on the knob as she eyed him suspiciously.

"Good Lord!" he growled, taking in the room before him. "Who the hell did your decorating?"

"I did. Sorry if it doesn't meet with your approval!"

"I didn't say that," he placated, moving toward a curious construction of bronze and wood that stood on a glass end table. "It just takes a little getting used to...."

She watched him as he touched the sculpture with a surprisingly sensitive hand. York was wearing a charcoal gray suit, and the overall effect of his midnight black hair, dark clothing, and intrinsic aura of danger made for a savage contrast to the nearly all-white apartment.

There was a reason for the plush white carpet, white walls, low, white leather furniture, and glass tables. The place had been specifically designed to form a backdrop for the amazing assortment of artwork that was displayed throughout the apartment. Huge, swirling shapes on canvases drenched with color hung on the walls while dazzling and often strangely shaped mobiles hung in the corners from the ceiling. Wildly designed pieces of sculpture occupied several places on the floor and on the wide glass coffee table.

"Do you, uh, charge admission to the gallery?" York asked wryly as he turned slowly to face her. One dark brow lifted behind the frames of his glasses.

In spite of herself, Selena's hazel eyes sparkled with humor. "Unfortunately I don't think I could convince very many people to pay to see most of this stuff!"

"You mean it's not just me and my uncultured tastes? Other visitors lack an appreciation of all this art?" York moved one hand in a flat arc to encompass the assortment around him.

"This," Selena announced, stepping firmly away from the door, "is a very personal collection."

"You did all these?" he asked in amazement.

"No, I'm not an artist. Everything you see here," she confessed ruefully, "is a gift."

"Some friends!"

"They are all the works of genuine artists, Mr. Sutherland," she corrected him loftily, sinking down onto the white sofa. Her brightly colored knit dress was an added swatch of color against the light background. "Please sit down," she added formally.

"Artists who happen to be a little ahead of their time?" he hazarded in amusement as he relaxed into the chair across from her.

At that her mouth quirked. "I'm afraid so. In a few cases I don't think the public will ever be ready for some of this, er, talent!" Her amused gaze went fondly to a purple-and-green canvas that hung on the opposite wall.

"So how did you end up with all of it?" he pressed bluntly.

"It's a little difficult to explain," she admitted slowly. "Most of the people who did these are customers at the store I manage, you see, and..."

"And you let them pay their bills by giving you samples of their work?" he demanded with the boundless disapproval of a true businessman.

"Hardly," she retorted. "Artistic Endeavors would have long since gone bankrupt if I'd adopted that sort of policy."

"So?"

Selena frowned. This really wasn't any of his business. What was she doing explaining the situation to him? "My store *does* have a policy of encouraging its clientele," she finally said coolly.

"I get it." York surprised her by nodding in immediate comprehension. "You mean, *you* have a policy of encouraging every struggling artist who comes along and they're so damned grateful for the moral support they repay you with some of their best efforts! You, in turn, haven't got the heart to chuck their endeavors into the trash! Instead you bring them home and find a place for them as if they were so many stray cats."

Selena blinked in astonishment. "How did you guess?" she asked weakly.

"It was rapidly becoming obvious as the facts piled up," he drawled with a hint of a grin. "And there's a certain softness in you that would contribute toward the situation."

"Softness!" she echoed coldly. "Mr. Sutherland, I'm not even going to ask what you mean by that." She sat forward assertively, striving to take command of the situation. "Largely because I don't care. Will you kindly state your business and be on your way so I can have my dinner?"

"York," he interposed gently.

"What?"

"Call me York. I think matters have gotten to that point at least, don't you? I haven't had my dinner yet, either." He smiled in what was probably meant to be an engaging way but which only served to make Selena more wary. "It's been a long, hard day. How about sharing a drink with me while I tell you my news?"

He was on his feet, pacing toward her kitchen, before Selena could think of a polite way to refuse the request. She turned helplessly on the couch to watch as he disappeared through the doorway and reappeared on the other side behind the breakfast bar.

"I would appreciate it if you would simply tell me whatever it is that's so important and take your leave!" she gritted as he found a bottle of Sonoma County Riesling chilling in the refrigerator.

"I need a drink," he told her flatly, pulling open drawers in the all-white kitchen, until he found the corkscrew. "What's more, you're going to need one, too."

"Are you here to inform me of a death in the family or the collapse of the stock market?" she inquired sarcastically.

"No, but what I have to say will signify a change in your future." He'd found a couple of long-stemmed wine glasses and was striding back toward the chair across from her.

Selena drew a long breath as she watched him pour out the wine. "I should never have let you inside the apartment,'' she said with quiet resignation as he handed her the glass. ''You're here to make trouble, aren't you?'' Their eyes met in a moment of silent, mutual assessment.

''No. I'm here to prevent it,'' he said evenly.

''You expect me to believe that after what happened last night?''

He went very still for an instant and then raised his glass in a silent, mocking salute. The corner of his mouth lifted a fraction. ''Did you find what happened last night...troubling?'' he murmured deeply.

''It's not polite to respond to a question with a question,'' she taunted, refusing to be trapped into an answer by the double-edged inquiry.

''I'm sure you're not surprised by my lack of manners. I think you have me pegged as a little uncivilized already, don't you?'' York sipped his wine, his whole attention apparently on the Riesling's bouquet.

Selena's mind made an intuitive connection. ''And because I've pegged you correctly, I'm a potential source of danger to you, aren't I?'' she breathed knowingly.

The long, dark lashes behind the glasses lifted as York glanced up to catch her narrowed gaze. ''Perhaps,'' he agreed cryptically.

"So it's not just a case of detaching me from Richard's side because of the element of psychological warfare involved. Taking me away from him would be a nice coup for you and would probably serve to annoy him for a while. But the real risk in not separating me from Richard is that eventually I may manage to convince him you really are dangerous. I might put him on guard before it's too late..." Her words trailed off as she struggled to imagine what harm this man could do Richard in a purely practical sense.

"I can make it worth your while to leave Anderson," York said with cool arrogance. Having tested the bouquet, he was now eyeing the pale gold color of his wine as if it were of supreme importance. He was clearly going to ignore her deduction and the ensuing charge.

"I should be insulted by that suggestion," Selena said grimly. "On the other hand, why should I bother acting outraged? It's only what I expected."

"No, there's no need to go through the exercise. I knew it wouldn't work in the first place." He nodded calmly.

"Then why did you make the attempt to bribe me?" she snapped angrily. It was going to be difficult hanging on to her temper around this man. Somehow, though, the prospect of losing it altogether seemed risky. He would find a way to use any lack of emotional control to his advantage. Selena wasn't sure how he could do so, but her intuition warned of the possibility. The man was dangerous and growing more so by the minute.

"I had to run through all the various approaches before I used the most ruthless one," York said, watching her with a level expression. "You literally ran from my arms last night and this evening you're refusing the bribe. Doesn't leave me much choice, does it?"

"You mean sex and money haven't worked so now you're going to drag out the really big guns?" she mocked, every instinct aware and alert and beginning to sound a warning. "You're bluffing, York. There's nothing left to try. I'm not going to abandon Richard for your doubtful charms or your money. Whatever made you think I'd be tempted by the latter, anyway?" she pressed, trying to score whatever small victory she could. "If I were shopping for a man who could guarantee me a tidy income, I chose right the first time, didn't I? You're doing very well for yourself, you're on the way up, but Richard has already arrived!"

"Ummm, that may be true," York agreed musingly, lounging back into the depths of the chair. It was uncanny, Selena reflected grimly, how her nervousness seemed to be increasing in direct proportion to the ease with which he was making himself at home! "The problem," he went on far too mildly, "is that while he may have arrived, so to speak, he can't make a place for you beside him up there at the top."

"What in the world are you talking about?" she demanded softly.

There was a small pause and then York said, each word a deliberate chip of ice, "He's married, Selena. And off hand I'd say there's almost no possibility of a divorce. I can prove it."

Three

———

Selena's gloved fingers were still shaking as she turned the key in the lock of the resort condominium in Utah a day later. She told herself it was from the cold. The adjustment from sunny Pasadena to the snow-covered mountains twenty miles outside of Salt Lake City was enough to make any civilized Californian shake, but honesty compelled her to admit that the involuntary response could still be attributed to sheer fury.

The scene with Richard Anderson had not been pleasant.

She'd owed him a chance to explain, a chance to deny the accusations York Sutherland had lodged, and Selena had given Richard that chance even though a part of her had known that Sutherland had been telling the truth. He wasn't the kind of man to resort to lies.

Neither man, she realized, could have estimated the explosive extent of her reaction. Finding oneself involved with a married man simply wasn't *that* uncommon in the state that prided itself in being on the cutting edge of the new morality. But neither man could have known how Selena's own marriage to a handsome, charming, quite brilliant artist named Cale Masters had crumbled because of "the other woman," a lovely young art student who truly "understood" Cale's temperamental nature. The thought of being made to play the role she despised so completely had infuriated Selena beyond even York's best estimates. Selena had empathized immediately with the unknown Mrs. Anderson.

York must have quickly sensed the potential of the force he had unleashed, however, because he hadn't hung around after dropping the bombshell. The near-green gaze had assessed the glittering fury in the eyes of his victim as she sat unnaturally still on the couch. Then he'd calmly taken a last sip of the expensive wine, risen lithely to his feet, and headed for the door with the satisfied air of a man who has set wheels in motion and who knows he need only wait until the inevitable has occurred.

Selena had called Richard the minute she'd slammed the door behind York.

"How did you dare?" she'd raged when he'd uncomfortably begun to admit the truth. "Who the hell do you think you are to do this to me? I will *not* be the other woman in any man's life! I will not allow you to use me in order to cheat on your wife. What made you think you could get away with it, Richard?"

Clearly taken aback by what he considered Selena's overreaction to the situation, Richard had tried to placate her, realizing too late that everything he said only got him in deeper and deeper.

"For God's sake, Selena, calm down!" he'd finally muttered desperately. "Elaine and I haven't even lived together for over a year...!"

"Are you telling me you're divorced?" she'd cut in challengingly.

"Well, no, not exactly..."

"Yes or no?"

"Selena, you have to understand," he'd pleaded. "There are reasons why a divorce isn't a...a solution at this point."

"Believe me, I'm not asking you to get one! I have no wish to be the reason you make the decision to leave your wife!" she'd retorted fiercely.

"Darling, I'd have left her months ago if it were possible," he'd nearly wailed. "You've got to listen to me, Selena. I don't know how you found out, but the reason I never told you about Elaine is because she simply isn't important to us! Compared to what you and I were finding together..."

"We've found nothing together! And furthermore, don't ever let me *find* you anywhere near me again!"

There had been more in the same vein before Selena had finally tossed the receiver back into its cradle with thoroughly disgusted violence. When she'd lifted it again, it was to call John and Louise Fletcher.

Neither had questioned her abrupt decision to make use of the ski resort condominium. They had been delighted to have her accept the invitation and had arranged at once to give her the key and directions. The next day, still simmering with the force of her anger, Selena had caught a plane to Salt Lake City.

Now here she was, stepping inside the luxurious vacation apartment, underdressed for the weather and not the least bit interested in learning how to ski. She glanced around at her surroundings with mild curiosity.

It was a one-bedroom arrangement, a bit on the small side, but beautifully furnished if you liked the standard subtle-toned modern look. There wasn't much personality to the place, she decided critically as she took in the light beige carpet, beige drapes, and the earth tones of the furniture. Only to be expected in a resort condominium that served a number of owners, she supposed as she tossed her purse down onto a light brown chair and walked over to the window.

There was no criticizing the view, however. Acres of snow-covered landscape stretched before her. From the vantage point of the second-floor unit she could watch the brightly dressed skiers whizzing down the slopes, and off to the left a chair lift carried others back to the tops of the various runs. Did all those people really enjoy being out in the cold?

The thought made her turn to the fireplace with determination. Nothing like a cheerful blaze to counter all that ice and snow! The firewood was stacked on the small, sheltered balcony. With only the protection of the overworked calfskin gloves, Selena pushed aside the wide sliding glass door and stepped out into the chill to collect a few chunky-looking logs. Good Lord! It was cold! She was shivering before she'd gathered what appeared to be a sufficient amount of firewood and she turned the electric heat up higher until the fireplace could assume the responsibility of heating the apartment.

A look inside the refrigerator revealed only empty shelves, and a glance at the clock showed it was probably too late to find a market. Well, she could stock up in the morning. Tonight she would investigate the facilities of the nearby lodge.

An hour later, dressed in a pair of snug jeans, a rakish, long-sleeved oxford-style shirt in turquoise, and stylish, high-heeled boots that were absolutely no protection against the snow, Selena belted on a hip-length leather jacket and started for the lodge. At the first step outside her condominium building she gritted her teeth and pulled up the collar of the jacket to frame her face. This was a vacation?

The outfit she wore comprised the warmest clothes she had been able to find in her closet, but it took only three seconds to realize that California chic wasn't much use in the battle against Utah cold. In addition to groceries tomorrow, she was going to have to shop for some warmer clothing if she intended to survive the next two weeks!

Two weeks in these Utah mountains. Was it worth it? The answer, Selena decided as she crunched her way precariously along the snowy path, was yes. If ever a woman had needed to get away from a depressing situation, it was herself.

The anger at Richard was not going to disappear overnight, nor was her dismay at her own failure to see through his lies. Her intuition was usually a reliable force. Why had it failed her this time? She had been used and she was human enough to entertain a few fleeting fantasies of revenge, knowing, of course, that she would have to content herself with having been the one to end the relationship.

Her feelings toward York Sutherland weren't any more charitable. Damn the man! He would literally do anything to win, she thought in bemused wonder. She'd sensed it from the first and his actions had proved it. The resentment she felt toward him seemed somehow stronger and more complex than her simple anger at Richard. The element of fascination she had been forced to acknowledge played a role in all this, she thought grimly.

Selena was still trying to analyze that one when she reached the entrance of the charmingly rustic ski lodge and stepped gratefully into the warmth of the heavily paneled and timbered building.

The huge circular fireplace in the center of the lobby drew her like a magnet and she went toward it at once, hands extended eagerly.

"You look a little chilled," observed a nearby male with a sympathetic chuckle.

"I'm not sure my feet are even still attached. I can't feel them at the moment," Selena groaned, stripping off the thin, unlined calfskin gloves and glancing ruefully down at her boots. When she looked up again, she favored the man across from her with a wry smile, sizing up his pleasant good looks. He was probably in his early thirties. The tousled blond hair, dark ski tan, warm brown eyes, and expensive designer label après-ski clothes gave the impression that he knew his way around the local territory.

"No offense, but you aren't exactly dressed for the environment, are you?" he replied amiably, returning the appraisal. "I'm Ty Loren, by the way. Just arrive?"

"Yes, as a matter of fact. It shows, does it?" Selena grimaced. "I flew in from California this afternoon on somewhat short notice..." She hesitated and then shrugged. "My name is Selena Caldwell."

"Don't worry, Selena. The shops here can supply you with anything you need tomorrow. What you need at the moment, however, is probably a hot toddy. Can I buy you one in the bar?" Ty waited hopefully.

She considered the offer. Ty Loren moved fast. Then again, what harm would there be in accepting a drink? A little easy company might be just the thing to take her mind off her problems. First things first, however. She flashed a brilliant smile.

"Only if you'll swear on your old Boy Scout honor that you are not now married, separated, engaged, or otherwise committed!"

Ty blinked in surprise and then grinned. "Cautious soul, aren't you? Never mind, you have my word I'm a free man. Can I get the same assurance from you?" he added a little carefully.

"You most certainly can," she told him in a heartfelt voice. "I'm a free woman."

With a pleased look, Ty took her arm and led her into the plush bar where another hearth promised further comfort. The feeling came back into Selena's chilled feet as she sank into one of the heavily upholstered chairs at a small round table.

"Here for a long visit?" Ty demanded after ordering the hot toddies.

"A couple of weeks, unless I freeze to death first. What about you?"

"Another few days and then it's back to the salt mines in San Francisco. I'm with a law firm there," he murmured, establishing his status with a suitably casual style. San Francisco lawyers vacationing at sophisticated ski resorts were bound to be accepted anywhere and he knew it.

Selena relaxed as the warmth of the room took hold and the hot toddy arrived. "This really isn't so bad," she told her newfound acquaintance consideringly, sipping at the drink as she eyed the darkening ski slopes outside the insulated windows. "As long as you're indoors, that is!"

"Ever ski before?"

"Nope. And I don't intend to start. I'm just here because some friends decided at the last minute that they wouldn't be able to use their condo this year."

The conversation was quickly becoming the friendly, casual kind and Selena didn't fight it. Where was the harm? Ty seemed pleasant company, and although she had no intention of actively encouraging him beyond the present level of association, Selena found herself willing to spend the evening with him. His cheerful, intelligent conversation was successfully taking her mind off the disturbing fury and dismay that still ran like a deep current beneath the surface of her thoughts. Being with him was rather like going out to an entertaining film when one was in need of diversion.

Wondering how Ty would feel if he could overhear her mental description of his usefulness brought a quirking curve to Selena's mouth as she lifted her thick glass mug once more.

As she did so she let her amused gaze idly sweep the room full of boisterous people who had spent the day on the slopes or were actively engaged in giving a good imitation of having done so. Here and there a white plaster cast caught the eye but even those unlucky skiers seemed quite cheerful. Where had she read that the broken bones of skiers tended to heal more quickly than similar injuries incurred in other ways? Nothing like a positive attitude, Selena reminded herself bracingly.

Her wandering gaze found the entrance to the lounge as that last thought crossed her mind. And became suddenly riveted. She nearly choked on her hot toddy as she took in the sight of the tall, dark shape in the doorway.

He *couldn't* have followed her here to Utah! Why on earth would York Sutherland do such a thing? She was, after all, of no further use to the man. Hadn't he won the battle in which she'd unwittingly become a pawn?

The mug in her hand came down on the table-top with a jarring sound and Ty glanced at Selena in surprise.

"Something wrong?" he asked with concern.

"You could say that," she agreed tartly. "Someone I know and had hoped not to run into again has just arrived."

It was too late to explain further. York had located her in the crowd and was starting toward the couple in the corner. Selena watched his lean, wolfish stride as if mesmerized by an advancing enemy. Time seemed to stand dangerously still for an instant before she could break the spell and drag her gaze back to Ty.

It didn't do much good. The image of York could not be erased from her mind's eye. He was wearing clothes as totally unsuited to the environment as she was, which made sense since he must have left on even shorter notice than she had!

Close-fitting jeans rode low on narrow hips, clasped by a heavy leather belt with a mean-looking bronze buckle. From somewhere far back in his closet he'd found a plaid flannel shirt. Other than the dark brown leather jacket he was unfastening as he crossed the room, the shirt was his only concession to the cold.

Snowflakes still glinted in the midnight blackness of his hair and he'd removed his glasses, probably in an attempt to keep them from being coated with melting snow. He was reaching for the frames inside the jacket even as he glided to a halt beside the table Selena was sharing with Ty.

The glasses were slipped into place with an automatic gesture, and cold green eyes looked down in the assessing glance Selena knew so well. York focused on her for a second as she was forced to look up in acknowledgment of his presence. Then the hawkish stare shifted to sweep dispassionately over a somewhat astonished and immediately alert Ty Loren.

"Would you mind," York said with the smoothness of a professional assassin, "if I had a private talk with my wife?"

Ty froze. "Your wife!" He snapped his head around to stare helplessly at Selena, who was gasping in astounded helplessness herself. "She said—" He tried again, "She said she was a...a free woman!"

"Sometimes they're the most expensive kind," York noted quietly, the gleaming green eyes sliding to Selena, who finally managed to untangle her tongue even though she had a strong hunch it was already too late. York had nearly routed the enemy with a blitzkrieg attack.

"Ignore him, Ty. He only exists to make trouble."

"Look," Ty was saying, choosing to ignore Selena instead, "there's some mistake. I didn't know she was married." He was getting to his feet, all apology to the jaguar who stood quietly beside the table. "No harm done. We just had a drink together. I only met her a short while ago...."

"I understand," York growled softly. "Goodbye."

Ty was gone, disappearing into the crowd with evident relief. Selena tossed an icy glance up at York and then pointedly rose herself.

"Since you've seen fit to end my evening a little earlier than I'd planned, I'll say good night and go home," she told him without any inflection whatsoever. Boldness was her only recourse. She moved to edge haughtily past him. She would not rage at the man; there was no point because he wasn't the sort to be intimidated by a woman's fury. Besides, Selena told herself cynically as the awareness of him washed in waves through her body, the highest priority at the moment was getting away from him.

But York had not won the first battle of the evening so easily only to lose the second. He reached out and caught hold of Selena's arm, effectively halting her escape.

"No," he grated a little huskily. "I came all this way to find you. I have to talk to you, Selena."

She looked back at him over her shoulder and let her carefully expressionless gaze slide down to where he gripped her arm. The heat and power of his hand anchored her as surely as a bond of steel.

"Be careful, York," she advised dryly. "In the old days they used to kill the messenger who brought ill findings. You've gotten away with it once. I don't recommend you press your luck. I'm not in the mood for any further revelations. In any event, you've done all the damage you need to do, haven't you? I'm out of the hostilities between you and Richard!"

"I have to talk to you," he retaliated. "Come on. Let's get out of here."

"I don't care where you go but you're going there by yourself."

"I won't ask for any suggestions as to the destination," he drawled, something easing in his voice as he forged a path through the lively crowd and pulled her after him.

An irresistible force, Selena thought with a savage sigh of resignation. The bite of frosty air made her catch her breath as they stepped outside. Beside her York swore in response.

"Damn! but it's cold here! Why the hell did you have to pick Utah?"

"Why the hell did you have to come after me?" she snapped back, finding the support of his hand suddenly useful as the icy walk became treacherous.

"I didn't have a choice."

Unwilling to demand further explanation, Selena kept her silence as they walked toward the modern two-story building that housed the condominium she was using.

"Which one?" York finally asked, drawing to a halt at the entrance of the structure.

"Which one what?" Selena retorted, determined not to be helpful.

"Which apartment? Listen, Selena, we can both stay out here and argue until we freeze to death in each other's arms or we can go inside and talk like civilized human beings. Take your choice!"

With a supreme effort of will, Selena controlled her blazing temper. It *was* cold, damn it!

"We'll go inside," she ordained caustically. "Freezing to death in each other's arms sounds a great deal more intimate than I would ever care to get with you!'' She stepped toward the doorway.

"Whew!'' York whistled behind her. "I take it all back. With you breathing fire like that maybe we wouldn't freeze to death out here after all.''

Selena refused to respond even though she could almost have sworn there was a hint of humor in his voice now. Wordlessly she led the way down the hall to the Fletchers' apartment and fished in her shoulder bag for the key.

"All right, York, say whatever it is you have to say. I'm on pins and needles waiting to hear what brought you all this way just to ruin my vacation. You're a rather ruthless man, aren't you? Not content with wrecking my relationship with Richard, you have to ruin the first time off I've had in a long while.''

She stepped inside the apartment, unconsciously relaxing a little in the welcome warmth. Swinging around on one booted heel, Selena planted her hands on her hips and glared at the man who had followed her inside.

York shut the door and faced her, a hooded, brooding glance raking her slender figure.

"Well?'' she demanded tautly. "What's this all about? How did you find me, anyway?''

"I've only been about an hour and a half behind you every step of the way. I found out where you intended to run from one of the clerks at Artistic Endeavors."

"I was not running!" She shut her eyes in a brief, silent plea for patience. "Forget that. A fruitless argument, I'm sure. Am I going to get an explanation for all this drama? There must be a clear-cut, very logical one. With you there always is. Tell me how I fit into your current battle plan and I'll do you the favor of getting out of it again. I would have thought I was well and truly out of the picture by now, though! You were quite successful, you know. I won't be having anything more to do with Richard Anderson. Easy, wasn't it? Did you know it would be that easy? I . . . York!"

His name was a startled gasp on her lips as he reached for her, pulling her into his arms with a demanding fierceness that cut off her tirade.

"The hell with it," York rasped. "Selena, I didn't come all this way just to listen to you yell at me for telling you the truth about Anderson!"

His hands slid up from her arms to wrap her throat possessively in still-cold fingers. Selena stared up at him, wide-eyed and so fully aware of him that she thought her senses must surely overload.

"Then why did you come?" she managed.

"I came for you," he told her with the frightening simplicity of a man who always gets what he wants.

"You can't have me!" He was so close. The heat of his body seemed to reach out to her, drawing her closer even as the beckoning flames of the fireplace in the lodge had earlier. "And I don't believe you, anyway," she added immediately, feeling a kind of pounding hysteria roaring through her veins. "You never really wanted me, you were out to ruin Richard! I was merely unlucky enough to get in the way!"

"For God's sake, Selena, don't you know you've been slowly driving me out of my mind for the past three weeks? Ever since I saw you with Anderson." He smothered an exclamation of impatience and the fingers around her throat tightened as he drew her closer. "Why am I trying to talk at this stage?" he asked himself half under his breath.

Selena shivered, realizing his intention and uncertain how to combat it. This man had been on her mind for the past three weeks, a growing shadow of menace and fascination that had finally coalesced into an all too tangible and dangerous form. She should have been actively fighting him and all she could think of was that she no longer owed any loyalty to Richard. She truly was a free woman at that moment. Free to step into York Sutherland's circle of sensual danger.

But the freedom of choice was being denied her. He wasn't waiting for her to come to him, he was reaching out and dragging her close, much too close. . . .

York lowered his head to take her mouth in a kiss of hungry ravishment that could not be denied. Selena's hands came up to push against the leather of the jacket he wore but the effort was appallingly useless. Her mind whirled with the overwhelming masculine desire being loosed upon her and she was stunned by her body's acceptance of that desire.

"I want you," York ground out against her mouth. "I've been wanting you for weeks! When I finally succeed in prying you away from Anderson, what do you do? Run off to Utah!"

"I wasn't . . . !"

Her muffled protest was drowned as he seized the advantage, thrusting his tongue aggressively between her lips. Selena groaned, her fingertips digging into the leather covering his shoulders.

"You don't paint pictures," she managed almost painfully as the front of her jacket fell open and his fingers slid inside to find the curve of her waist, "you make battle plans and plot campaigns. I won't be part of your warfare, York Sutherland!"

The small smile faded as he took in her earnest refusal to believe his words.

"You think you have me all figured out, don't you?" he whispered throatily, swinging her abruptly up into his arms and carrying her across the room to the low couch. There he sank heavily down, holding her across his thighs. When she tried to right herself and slide off his lap, his arm closed about her in an absent gesture, pinning her.

"It doesn't take any great degree of perception to understand how your mind works," she retaliated softly. "I've known from the first what you wanted."

Almost warily he raised a hand and removed his glasses, setting them down on the table beside the couch. The thick black lashes closed as he leaned back into the corner of the cushions. Selena was suddenly struck by the realization that he was tired. The tiny sign of human weakness in him had an unexpected softening effect on her. She supposed even experienced assault commanders got tired occasionally. It had been a long day for both of them.

But when the ebony lashes lifted fractionally and she saw the fully alert gleam in the gray-green eyes, Selena changed her mind. The man wasn't succumbing to exhaustion, he was merely assessing the situation further.

"What is it you think I want, Selena?" he challenged gently. Too gently. She didn't trust the velvet in his voice.

"I'm not sure," she admitted cautiously. "You've already achieved your primary goal, which was to take me away from Richard. Perhaps that wasn't sufficient. Perhaps your need to win requires that you demonstrate to him that you can not only force me away from him, you can make me want you instead."

He regarded her through narrowed lids. "Can I make you want me?"

Selena flinched at the blunt question. "You're not nearly as intelligent as I've assumed you are if you think I'd answer a question like that!"

Humor flickered briefly in the set features of his face. "A little bit on the loaded side, hmmm?"

"If I said no, you can't make me want you, I'd become a challenge. If I said yes, you'd take advantage of the situation, wouldn't you?" she braved.

"Probably," he agreed, lifting his hand to stroke back the line of her chestnut hair. "Selena, you're right about my goals," he went on evenly.

Selena held herself steady against the impact of hearing the truth admitted. Deep down, had she really wanted him to deny it?

"But you're wrong about my motives," he concluded flatly. "I want you but not because I'm trying to use you in my war against Anderson."

"It just happens that things will work out that way very nicely if you get me, is that it?" she taunted fiercely, trying to maintain a bold front in the face of his newest attack. "How dare you insult my mental capacity by implying that this great passion you've conceived for me didn't have its roots in the fact that I was dating Richard!"

"I can't deny that if I hadn't been out to get Anderson I probably wouldn't have even met you. That's a straightforward fact," he began carefully.

"And you can't deny that your initial interest in me was based on the idea that I could be used in your game plan!"

"I could, but I won't, because you obviously wouldn't believe me," he tossed back coolly.

"Tell me the truth, York!" she demanded bitterly.

He hesitated. "Selena, the only thing that matters tonight is that I want you, and I think, if you're honest with yourself, you want me." He touched her lips with the edge of his finger when she opened her mouth to argue. "Please don't refuse to admit we're attracted to each other. That much I can force from you and we both know it. If you insist on pushing me, I might lose my patience and resort to doing exactly that."

She lifted her chin in defiance. She knew she couldn't deny the fascination she felt for him, but she could demand a price for admitting it. "I suggest we both exchange a little honesty," she bit out tightly. "Tell me the full truth about why you became interested in me and I'll admit what you want to hear!"

"You're trying to hurt both of us," he muttered raspingly.

"I can take it," she flung back boldly. "It's worth it for some genuine honesty!"

"The kind of honesty you never had from Anderson?" he said, slipping in the knife with practiced ease.

That particular truth struck a sensitive nerve. "Exactly!" she whispered furiously. "I broke off my relationship with him the moment you walked out of my door last night, York. Does that give you any satisfaction? Your tactics were entirely and totally effective. I'll never see him again."

She saw the satisfaction in his face, felt it in the arm that tightened around her body. His hand splayed possessively along her thigh. "Thank God for that much, at least," he growled.

"But," she raged on, keeping her tone low with an incredible effort, "I'm not about to replace one lying male with another! So tell me the truth, damn it!"

"What does it matter why I first decided I had to have you? The end result is the same, you little fool. There's another side to the coin, you know. If you hadn't sensed I was out to crush the man you were with, you wouldn't have tried so hard to ignore me. If you'd been honest with me and with yourself, you wouldn't have run from me! You didn't owe him any loyalty, Selena, surely you can see that now...."

"Oh, yes, I can see it," she cried furiously. "You made certain I learned the full truth, but don't expect me to thank you for it!"

"Are you longing for Anderson, Selena?" he demanded harshly.

"No! How could I long for a liar and a cheat? I wouldn't waste my time. He tried to make me play a role I once swore I would never get involved with and I'll never forgive him for that. He was no better than the man I married three years ago. And neither are you!"

"You're really out for blood tonight, aren't you?" he breathed in a wondering voice, the green of his eyes turning very hard. "The question is, who are you going to wind up drawing it from? Me or yourself? You want an admission that the first time I saw you I wanted to take you away from Anderson? You've got it. I'll freely admit it. You want me to say that the reason I wanted to take you away from him was because I saw it as a small, psychological victory over the man that would eventually make the final win all the sweeter? You've got it. I admit it. But the admissions stop there, Selena. I didn't kiss you that night on the hotel terrace because of Richard Anderson. I kissed you because I wanted you for myself. The same reason I followed you to Utah and the same reason I'm going to make love to you tonight! There, are you satisfied?"

Selena fought for control of her voice and her emotions. She'd wrenched the truth out of him at last and he was right, she'd drawn a little blood in the process. He'd acknowledged that his initial interest in her had been because of her association with Richard Anderson. Why did the information hurt? She'd known it all along! But had he truly followed her because he now wanted her for himself? Was she no longer merely a pawn but the goal in his war game? An exciting thrill coursed through her body, a thrill she could not deny.

"Thank you for the honesty," she got out regally, hazel eyes veiled behind her lashes as she tried to hide the conflicting emotions racing along her nerve endings. "But if *everything* you said was the truth," she continued softly, "if you really came to Utah because you want me for yourself—"

"I did and I do," he interrupted equally softly, fingers toying tantalizingly along the line of her throat.

"Then you're in for a small disappointment," she wound up staunchly. "You're not going to make love to me tonight, York Sutherland, regardless of what brought you here!"

The tension in him communicated itself to her even before he spoke. "I'm going to make love to you, Selena." His voice was deep and steady and held all the certainty in the world. "I have to make love to you. It's the only way."

"The only way to do what?" she gasped, unnerved.

"The only way to make you understand how much I want you, the only way to prove to you how much you want me. You're going to fight me every inch of the way until I have you in my bed. Don't you think I know that? You'll find excuses, drag your feet, think of reasons why you should put off giving yourself to me. You're scared of me and I don't know any other way of getting around that fear except by taking you to bed and forcing you to face the truth about us."

"You're out of your mind if you think I'd let you treat me like that!" she exclaimed, horribly conscious of her vulnerable position there in his lap. "I'm not some nervous filly you can break to the saddle by sheer force!"

His mouth quirked at the image and something softened in his eyes. "You're telling me you expect to be slowly wooed and won?"

"If there's any possibility of a . . . a long-term relationship between us, York Sutherland, it can only develop out of a gradual process of getting to know each other. Frankly I don't think there's much hope," she tacked on waspishly in an effort to counter the humor in his eyes. "But that's the only way I'm even willing to consider going about it!"

"Just look how far you've come already tonight," he murmured persuasively, touching the pulse at the base of her throat lightly. "When you first saw me this evening, you were furious, and now here you are discussing the terms of a possible relationship."

"Pointing out your various victories as you go along is hardly the way to my heart!" she blazed in response, all too well aware of how far she had slipped since he'd first walked into the lounge.

"Thank you for the advice," he said in a deep voice, letting his fingers glide down her skin to the opening of the turquoise shirt. "I'll keep it in mind."

"You're laughing at me!" she accused.

"A little. You think you've got me all psyched out, all my motives categorized and understood..."

"And I don't?"

"No." He shook his head once, slowly. "Perhaps you will, though, after I've taken you to bed with me."

"I'm not going to bed with you, York," Selena said very steadily, secretly proud of her stamina in the face of his persistence. Was this how he won his battles? By pushing without any let-up until he had reached his goal?

"Why not?" he drawled persuasively, lowering his head to put his lips at the point he had been teasing with his fingers.

"Because you'd only view it as a . . . a form of surrender!" Selena could barely manage to get the words out. Her eyes squeezed tightly shut as the light, licking fire of his kiss penetrated into her blood.

"Would surrendering to me be so bad, sweetheart?" She could feel his teeth in a tiny, exciting nip at the curve of her throat and shivered.

"It would make you the winner," she whispered wretchedly.

"Don't think of it in those terms," he coaxed, unfastening the first white button on the turquoise shirt.

"I have to think of it in those terms because that's the way you think of it!" she protested.

"Selena," he begged, voice hardening as he kissed the gentle upper swell of her breast, "give yourself to me tonight. Come to me. *Surrender* to me and I swear you won't regret it. Afterward I'll give you all the time you need, I'll woo you properly, if that's what you want. But first I need to know you're mine. I need to know you've accepted me completely and that there won't be any other men in your life."

Selena stirred restlessly against him, not knowing if she was seeking a way to be free or a way to meld more closely into his warmth. She was being seduced and she knew it, knew her body was absorbing the growing impact of him with rising need and desire. What was it about this man that seemed to fascinate her senses so much? It was uncanny. There had never been another man like him in her life.

"York, no. The answer is no. It has to be!"

"Let me show you the pictures I've been painting in my dreams, darling Selena," he said huskily. "You're the collector who has a place in her home for the artwork of all those dreaming artists you encourage. Make a place for me. Please, Selena."

Her head sank down onto his shoulder, her hands clinging to him as the tide of battle began to go against her. She had known from the beginning that her body was weak and would probably go down easily in the face of his advance, but she had thought her mind could hold out against him. With mental barriers firmly in place she had hoped to protect her far weaker body. But it appeared that mind and body were irrevocably connected and shared the same susceptibility to the kind of campaign York was waging.

"Something tells me you wouldn't be content with a place on the wall or the end table," she sighed. "You would want to dominate the whole gallery!"

"Yes," he said, not bothering to deny it.

Selena shut her eyes once again as he gathered her more securely to him. "I knew it," she muttered. "The answer is no, York. I won't go to bed with you tonight."

"That's it, sweetheart," he approved tenderly, surging strongly to his feet with her in his arms. "Close your eyes and don't think about it. Don't think about it until morning."

Selena felt herself being borne across the beige carpet, carried off into the night by a sleek and savage jaguar. By morning it would be too late.

Four

"It won't do you any good without the words, York," Selena said challengingly as he carried her into the beige-and-brown bedroom with its king-size bed.

"Your surrender?" he clarified, not pretending to misunderstand as he set her down gently on the tan quilt. He swept the shape of her with a shuttered glance. "It would be better with the words, I'll give you that," he went on half-musingly as he shrugged out of his leather jacket and let it fall to the floor. Then the edge of his mouth lifted in silent humor. "But we starving artists can't be too choosy, can we? I'll take what I can get for now. The words can come later.''

She wanted him. How she wanted him! Her senses had been filled with the awareness of him since they had first met, and he seemed to know that. She had fought the attraction of him and probably would have been able to go on fighting it if he hadn't chosen to overwhelm her like this. But of course he had chosen this method. York Sutherland knew tactics.

He sat down on the bed beside her and Selena instinctively tucked her legs beneath her, kneeling in a position that suggested flight at any moment. Seeing that, York reached out, caught her lightly around the waist, and tumbled her down onto her back. Her chestnut hair fanned out on the quilt.

''Didn't you guess I'd come after you?'' he asked thickly as he sprawled across her and cupped her face between rough palms. ''Tell me the truth.''

''No,'' she denied, her pulses pounding in response to the weight of his body on hers. ''How could I have guessed?''

''And you thought you had me so thoroughly pegged,'' he scoffed, lowering his head to seal her mouth with his own.

This time his kiss was a slow, drugging caress that swept her into a whirlpool. She moaned into his mouth and he drank the sound of implicit surrender with masculine eagerness. His hand moved under the edge of the blue-green shirt and found the tip of her unconfined breast. It budded to life at his touch, and Selena felt the tautening sensation radiating deep into her thighs.

Slowly, with compelling urgency, York undressed her, rising for a moment to tug off her heeled boots and jeans. When she lay beneath his gaze wearing only the now-opened shirt and delicate lace panties, he went to work on his own clothes. His eyes never left her and he kept one palm moving with teasing roughness across her breasts and over the slope of her stomach as he tugged off his flannel shirt and unclasped the belt at his waist.

The hand he kept on her was a chain, Selena knew. It was a bond that maintained the link he was establishing while he prepared to strengthen that link with the act of physical possession. She watched him from beneath heavy lashes as he peeled away his clothing, presenting himself boldly to her gaze.

And her artistic eye found a seductive pleasure in the sight of him. She could not deny it. Before she could stop herself, she lifted a hand

and trailed questioning fingertips across his shoulder and down through the tapering, curling hair on his chest. He was lean and supple, and the strength in him was incredibly enticing to the feminine core of her. The dangerous fascination was flowing around her, making the possibility of escape uninteresting.

"The wanting has just about driven me crazy during the past few weeks," he told her hoarsely, catching hold of her questing hand and stilling it as it dropped to his thigh. "Every time I saw you throw away your smiles on Anderson, I felt like kidnapping you and taking you away to a place where there would be only me to smile at. You have the most beautiful smile, sweetheart, full of warmth and gentleness. And you seemed to smile at everyone but me!"

Selena couldn't help it. The smile he seemed so enthralled with touched her lips. "Braces," she confided.

Incomprehension replaced the emerald fires of his eyes just as he was bending to kiss the hardening crest of her breast. "Braces!"

"I wore them for two years. Cost my parents a fortune. I'm sure they would be delighted to know you like the resulting smile!"

Nothing of the passion in him dimmed, yet Selena could have sworn she felt him relax in some manner as he studied the hesitant humor in her gaze. A slow, wicked grin curved across his face. "What happens if I praise the glowing gold of your blue-and-green eyes?"

A strange tingle of relief spread through Selena as he responded to the banter. "Why, then I tell you about the contact lenses I'm wearing," she murmured.

He nodded, eyes glinting as he deliberately drew a path down her breast to her hip. "Anything else I ought to know about?" he demanded meaningfully.

"Oh, no. Everything else is the real me!" she assured him throatily, aroused by the flash of humor that had entered the heavy desire that was permeating the room. In a way she couldn't describe there was a kind of reassurance about it. If York had seldom seen her smile during the past three weeks, it was equally true that she had rarely witnessed his. The danger in him was still unarguably present, but Selena suddenly thought she could handle it as long as there was a gentler side.

She had better be able to handle it, she thought fleetingly as he drew her closer, tangling his strong, teasingly rough legs with her silky ones, because there was no way she could halt the onslaught tonight.

"The real you is what I came all this way to find," York assured her in a voice of thickest velvet.

"Is that…" Selena touched her lip with the tip of her tongue and tried again. "Is that the only reason you came after me?" she breathed tremulously, searching his face for hidden meanings.

"The only reason."

She sighed in acceptance of the night and what it would bring, her arms going around him as York bent his head to her throat with a groan of desire. The only reason. If the fascination was mutual, surely there was hope?

The tips of her bronze-toned nails began to draw designs of passion over the thrusting contours of his back. The primitive artistry was an instinctive response to the sensual patterns he was weaving on the canvas of her body. Selena's breath caught in her throat as York strung a trail of heated, damp kisses from the small bones of her shoulder to the aching peaks of her delicate breasts.

There his mouth stayed to tease and pet and excite until the devastating ache of need spread out into the farthest reaches of her body, bringing it fully alive and aware of the only man who could now satisfy it.

"Touch me, Selena," he pleaded roughly, guiding one of her fluttering hands down his chest, over the flat, male nipple and beyond. "I've wanted to know your touch!"

"York, oh, York!" she gasped huskily as he pressed himself testingly against her thigh. She felt the undeniable force in him and it sent ripples of excitement through her. The reckless fascination grew and grew within her.

The obvious depths of his desire for her deepened the element of wonder. No man, not even her ex-husband, had wanted her with this elemental, raging need. To be wanted so badly was an incredible seduction in and of itself, she realized, shaken. Whatever his motives, there could be no doubt of the honesty of York's longing for her. To have come all this way for *her!*

"I can hardly believe I've finally got you in my arms and that this time you won't be running away," he grated against the skin of her stomach. His hand traced caressing circles across her hip, down to her knee, and began to work slowly back up the inside of her thigh.

"Oh!" Selena moaned as York tantalized and provoked with the thrilling patterns he was making. She arched against the pressure of his hand and he leaned more heavily across her, letting his greater weight impress itself on her body. It was a preliminary action, a way of making her aware of the impending culmination.

"Tonight you are the canvas and I am the artist," he promised softly. "I will put my colors, my designs, my signature, on you. I won't leave any blank spaces for any other man to come along and fill. You will be completely mine!"

The harsh possession in his words seeped through the layers of sensual excitement, eliciting a faint warning, a warning Selena knew she should be heeding. Always the fascination she had known around this man had been tempered with that sense of warning. But tonight she couldn't do anything about it. It was all out of her hands. The slender, curving length of her wanted to know the imprint of him.

"Sometimes," she managed with deliberate provocation, "the artist loses control and the colors become wild and chaotic. The canvas wins because it demands more than the artist can give."

"Is art a battle, then?"

"Oh, yes," she vowed, threading her fingers through his heavy black hair with delicious languor. "Art is definitely a battle."

"Then I will win it."

Selena was unable to answer that and instead a low moan issued from far back in her throat as he drew a lacy pattern over the most sensitive part of her. It was almost more than she could bear and she turned her face convulsively toward his chest and sank her teeth a little savagely into his skin.

"York!"

He grunted huskily at the small pain she inflicted and punished her deliciously by increasing the tempo of the brush strokes he was making with his fingers. She lifted her hips, begging for more of him, but he held back a while longer, choosing to explore the smoothness of her skin with his lips.

"Every inch of you," he told her. "I want to cover every inch of you with my work." Sliding down the length of her body, he rained kisses from her breast to her ankles and then began a slow, surging glide back up.

At every point along the way he impressed the print of his warm mouth on her skin. His fingers caressed, painted, brushed. Selena was tingling with the effects of his thorough lovemaking by the time he had made a path back to her small breasts. In the process he had forged a place for himself between her thighs until now he rested heavily along the entire length of her.

"Tell me you want me, Selena, darling," he ordered roughly as she writhed beneath him.

"Tell me you need me tonight as much as I need you!"

She moved her legs lightly along his, glorying in the feel of him, and her arms curved lightly around his neck. "I want you, York. You must know that by now!" Did the canvas have to beg for the artist's touch?

"Sweetheart!"

She could feel him pressing against her slowly, tentatively, as if waiting for her reaction to the prospect of his final intrusion. He nipped tiny, sandpapery kisses across her shoulders and held her hips tightly with clenching hands.

Urgently Selena beckoned him with her body, needing him completely. Still he teased and tantalized until she was crying out his name over and over again, begging, pleading, surrendering.

At last he seemed satisfied, and when her nails moved encouragingly on the taut skin of his shoulders one more time, he responded by finally taking her body by storm.

"Selena!" Her name was a hoarse cry from deep in his chest as he swept into her and captured her completely.

As for Selena, she couldn't even find her voice in that moment. The line between assault and art was very fine, indeed. Why had she never had that flaring realization before? The colors of the universe flowed through her, singing in her blood as York established the ancient rhythm.

Lost in his arms, she gave herself up to the forces he was unleashing, clinging to him as he filled her with bright patterns. It was unlike anything she had ever known.

The rhythm gradually began to increase as York sought to merge the artist and his art. At times he appeared to attack the canvas; at other times he caressed it with the lightest of brush strokes, but always he deepened the meld until all sense of time was dissolved.

The sparkling, light-filled hues became unbearably bright for Selena, her body tightening with a tension that could only be released by the man above her.

"York, oh, York! I can't ... I'm going to..." There were no words to describe what was happening and she clutched at him even more tightly.

"Let go, Selena," he gritted into her throat. "Let go and give in to it. Give in to *me!* I'll take care of you!"

The coaxing words were all it took to send her over the edge. The coiling tension reached the breaking point and exploded within and around her. Selena cried out wordlessly as her body shivered uncontrollably. She stopped breathing for an instant and then she was gulping for breath.

"My God! My God!"

York hurled out the exclamation that was also a talisman. His body tightened abruptly, arching forcefully, and then he was joining in the explosion of color and pattern.

Slowly, cautiously, gently, still holding tightly to each other, York and Selena collapsed in a meshed tangle of damp sheets and skin. For a long time they lay curled together, neither contemplating anything other than the languor of contentment and total relaxation. Finally Selena lifted her lashes, aware that York had not yet left her body. She found him braced lightly on his elbows above her, watching her. Masculine satisfaction radiated from his eyes and was etched into the harsh planes of his face.

"Don't look so... so victorious or I will strangle you," she whispered with gentle humor.

"Victorious?" York repeated thoughtfully, lowering his head to drop a little kiss on the tip of her nose. "I'm not sure that's quite the right word."

"No? What is the right word?" she challenged dreamily.

"What does any painter feel when the painting has been completed?"

"You tell me."

York smiled deliberately. "Satisfaction and anticipation," he proclaimed. "Satisfaction with the conclusion of the project and anticipation at the thought of doing it all over again very soon."

"You seem to have become quite an authority on art lately."

"All I want to do is become an authority on you," he murmured softly.

"Aren't you an authority after this?"

Something flickered in the depths of the gray-green eyes, something unfathomable and deep. He ducked his head and kissed the slope of her breast in a manner that was both reverent and profoundly sensual. Then he lifted his head again and regarded her soberly. "I think a man could spend a lifetime learning a woman as well as I want to learn you."

A surge of happiness washed over Selena's senses. He meant it, she was certain of it. He wanted her and perhaps, just perhaps, she had been wrong in her assumptions about him. Was it possible that York Sutherland knew how to love?

Selena tasted the word. Love. Slowly, surely, it began to replace the word "fascination" in her mind. It was a far better description of what she was feeling at the moment. The fascination that had been building for the past three weeks had blossomed into love here in his arms. In many ways it was still a fragile thing of crystal and fire, but there was no doubting the fundamental difference in the emotion.

"Does this mean you don't view tonight's events in terms of win and lose, surrender and victory?" she asked, trying very hard to keep her voice light and lilting. It wouldn't do for him to know how wary she had been of him, even while she was letting herself be seduced.

"You were the one who kept putting those words in my mouth," he pointed out, stroking the edge of her lips with his thumbs in a small, inviting caress.

"They weren't accurate?" she countered.

"Does it matter?"

"It matters." She met his eyes levelly, unwilling to back down. It did matter, damn it!

His mouth firmed. "Selena, you gave yourself to me tonight. That's the only fact that has any importance for either of us. I've wanted you for weeks and now you're mine. Forget anything else and concentrate on that."

"York, I think we should talk. So much has happened so quickly..."

"Later," he whispered huskily. "We'll talk later...."

She realized he was beginning to move within her, filling her, stoking the flames he had doused several moments earlier. She looked at him, wide-eyed and a little tremulous at the passionate strength in him.

He saw her expression, and the wicked challenge of his answering grin made her swallow hastily. "There are a few sections of my masterpiece that I want to go over again," he explained. "Some touch-up work."

Selena awoke hours later to the clarity of a mountain dawn. She lifted drowsy lashes and yawned, knowing the bright, dazzling sunlight bouncing off the snow wouldn't last long. A new storm was due this evening according to the weather forecasts.

She stirred and felt the warmth of the male body next to her. As she turned to look at York's sleeping figure the night's memories came back, bringing a light flush to her cheeks. It was unbelievably thrilling simply to lie there and look at him sprawled so at ease in her bed. The sheets had slipped to his waist and the contrast of his strong, tanned back against the crisp whiteness of the fabric was a potent eye-opener. She loved him.

Slowly, carefully, Selena reached out to touch the tousled blackness of his hair, toying with it for a moment before trailing her fingers down the length of his spine. At the swell of the muscular hip she stopped her exploration and waited expectantly.

He didn't move. Perhaps he was a sound sleeper. Or maybe he had exhausted himself with the extent of his own desire, she told herself in humorous satisfaction. Serve him right if he had. He had certainly exhausted her! She turned on her side and the shift of her weight reinforced the last notion. My God! She seemed to have developed muscles she hadn't even known she'd had! The faint soreness here and there was pleasant in a way. It wasn't that she was feeling masochistic, but the physical sensations emphasized the overwhelming memories of the night.

Watching his magnificently flung form, Selena grew impatient and began to make small circles at the sensitive base of his spine. Still no response. Craftily, a tiny, expectant grin shaping her lips, she teased the line of his thigh. Still he slept on like a huge, unworried cat.

Kneeling beside him now, Selena deliberately pushed the sheet aside and began to extend the range of her exploration. When she reached the soles of his feet, the bed seemed to explode around her.

"York!" she squeaked as he came awake in an incredible hurry. "Wait! I didn't mean it! How was I to know you were ticklish?"

"That was no lover's caress on the bottom of my foot!" He was sitting up, tossing the sheet over her head and bundling her into it before she could escape from the bed. He held his wriggling, captured prey in the sack formed by the bedclothes and hit the carpet with both feet.

"What are you doing?" yelped Selena from inside her prison. She could feel herself being carried across the room and was torn between laughter and the need to free herself. "Put me down this instant! York, I was only teasing...."

"Oh, I realize that," he assured her cheerfully.

"York, what's going on? Where in the world... No!"

The shower spray poured over her, sheet and all, cutting off her muffled protests. "York! The sheet!"

He set her on her feet and stripped the soaking material from around her. She looked up to meet his laughing eyes, finding him in the shower with her.

"It'll dry." He grinned, dropping the sheet in a heap in the corner of the wide stall shower. "And so will you. But not until I get an apology, woman!"

"For what?" she retorted, reaching up to wrap her arms around his neck as the water poured over both of them. "I was merely caressing you...."

"Tickling me, you mean."

"A fine line, apparently, with you."

"Nevertheless, one you're going to learn if I have to beat you regularly for a while," he informed her grandly. York molded her slick body to his own, his hands sliding to the rounded shape of her buttocks.

"Threats? After only one night in my bed?" she mocked sadly.

"I can't think of a better time to begin making them. Start as you mean to go on, they always say. Now about that apology...?"

"Apologies are so humiliating. Any chance I can make up for my faux pas in some other fashion?" she asked innocently, sliding her hips along his wanton provocation.

"What a sassy little flirt you are," he observed in a tone that was much too velvety.

"You bring out the worst in me, I'm afraid," she sighed woefully.

"Just make sure I'm the only one who witnesses the worst in you!" He gave her earlobe a none too gentle bite. "Where's my apology?"

"You want me to grovel?"

"Ummm. An interesting thought."

"I'm starving," Selena announced ingenuously. "I never did get dinner last night, thanks to you. Can't wait for breakfast."

"Don't change the subject. There won't be any breakfast for you until I get that apology." York reinforced the threat by delivering a stinging little slap to her rear.

"Ouch! Okay, okay! For the prospect of food, I'll apologize. Never again will I awaken you by tickling the soles of your feet!" She waited until she saw the catlike gleam of satisfaction in his eyes. "Unless, of course, I've got a clear shot at escape!"

"You," he told her, his voice suddenly losing all traces of humor, "will never escape me. Don't even think about the possibility. You're mine now."

Selena felt the abrupt change of mood in him, sensed the tightening of his grasp, and knew the words to be heavy with meaning.

"York?" she questioned a little uneasily.

But he forestalled the unasked portion of the query by sealing her mouth with his own in a kiss that proclaimed last night's possession in no uncertain terms.

In it Selena was fleetingly afraid that she tasted her own surrender and that which was carved on the other side of the coin: York's victory.

Five

___

"How long had you planned to hide up here in the mountains?" York inquired easily over breakfast in the lodge dining room.

"I was not hiding!" Selena exclaimed, not for the first time, in exasperation. She pointed her knife at him menacingly for a moment before going back to the task of spreading jam on her English muffin. "I came up here for a well-deserved vacation and I intended to stay two weeks. I still intend to stay two weeks," she finished loftily. Then she found herself waiting with barely concealed eagerness for him to say he would stay with her.

"You're not exactly prepared for the weather, are you?" York eyed her jeans and long-sleeved white shirt critically. The fine leather boots had dried out overnight but they still felt stiff and uncomfortable this morning.

"I'll buy some cold-weather things this morning."

"You don't ski, either," York went on conversationally, taking a huge bite out of the pile of hash brown potatoes on his plate. He appeared ravenous this morning. Or perhaps he was always ravenous, Selena reflected kindly. It would take a fair amount of food to keep a jaguar going. Besides, she was a little hungry herself.

"I do a great job of sitting by a fire and drinking hot toddies while watching crazy skiers out on the slopes, though." She smiled brightly.

Selena wasn't altogether certain why she was making things difficult for York. But this morning, when she'd discovered he expected her to turn right around and head back to Pasadena with him, she had found herself rebelling. It was a gentle rebellion, to be sure, but a firm-minded one. Some intuition was urging her to stay here in Utah and make York stay with her. They needed the next two weeks together without the disruptions of the business and pressures waiting back in Pasadena.

So far York's arguments had been casual and logical, even mildly humorous, but he intended that they should leave for Pasadena now that he had achieved his goal. Selena resisted the small compulsion to chew on her lip while she tried to analyze the situation. He had come after her because he wanted her, she reminded herself, not because he was still trying to use her in the war against Richard Anderson.

She could not doubt the genuine passion in him, not after last night, but the discussion that had begun over breakfast was making her uneasy. A man did not change his whole character overnight, even if he was falling in love....

Automatically Selena made herself push that particular word out of her head. She was in love, but she had no real way of knowing how deep York's emotions ran. At this point in time she had better stick with the facts. York wanted her intensely; she was certain of that much. The word "love" had best be reserved for a later date.

"You came here on pretty short notice," he was remarking casually, pouring cream into his coffee. "Surely there were a lot of things you left hanging fire in Pasadena? What about the art store you manage?"

"It'll survive for a couple of weeks without me." He wanted to go back and he was trying to manipulate her into agreeing that it was the right decision. "I'm going to stay the two weeks, York."

He cocked an eyebrow at the determination in her low voice and sipped his coffee in meditative silence. Selena hid her uneasiness behind a cheerful facade that was becoming more and more difficult to maintain. She barely tasted the food she was eating as she waited tensely for him to decide to go back to Pasadena on his own. Would she really be able to let him do that if he gave her an ultimatum? Selena's inner wince was almost painful. Already she sensed she would give in and return to California if that was the way York insisted on doing things.

But the feeling that they needed these two weeks together was strong. Her intuition again, she thought dryly. Something told her they needed this time together.

"Am I invited to stay here with you?" York stunned her by finally asking in a quiet tone.

She met his eyes across the table, happiness welling up inside. "Oh, yes, York, you're invited. I would like that very much!"

He smiled slowly. "How can I resist the welcome in your eyes?" He chuckled warmly. "I accept your invitation."

"It's the contact lenses," Selena told him modestly. "They add a certain sparkle."

"I prefer to think it's the memory of last night that is adding the sparkle." He grinned outrageously. "And no lectures on the extent of my ego, please. Surely a man's entitled to a little, er..."

"Preening?" Selena supplied artlessly. She ignored the laughter in his eyes. "You got what you wanted last night, didn't you?" she went on thoughtfully. "Do you always get what you want?"

"I'm not about to answer that," he informed her with smiling arrogance as he reached for the insulated coffeepot the waitress had left on the table. "Here, have another cup of coffee. You're going to need the warmth if you're bound and determined to stay in this snow country!"

He had gotten what he'd come after last night, but she had won a concession from him this morning, Selena told herself several times as they left the lodge and went in search of shops selling warm clothing. York hadn't intended to stay but he was going to do so.

She wasn't certain she liked the implication of a trade-off, however. It suggested a balance of power in the relationship, which disturbed her. On the other hand, knowing what she did about

York Sutherland, perhaps that was the only safe way to manage the affair! Damn it! She hadn't expected real love to become a game of power politics!

Calm down, she told herself as she selected a pair of fur-lined boots and a down jacket in a brilliant shade of yellow. You're overreacting, my girl. If all this had occurred with any other man, you wouldn't have thought twice about the situation. You would have understood his decision to return to Pasadena and acquiesced to it.

What it really came down to, of course, was that it was impossible to imagine herself in this sort of situation with any other man. When you fell overwhelmingly in love, it was difficult to think of the possibility of feeling such intense emotions with any other man on earth.

"Now what?" York demanded cheerfully as they headed back to the condominium with their purchases. "Are we going to go build a snowman? After an investment like this we'd better get some use out of these clothes!"

"I've got an idea! Why don't we buy a sled? Surely a couple of Southern Californians could learn to maneuver that!"

"You realize that the more money we pour into this vacation of yours, the more we're going to feel obliged to come back every year!'' he complained good-naturedly.

But they wound up buying the sled anyway, and after lunch they went in search of a moderate-size hill. There, after a few false starts and with the assist of several kids who were using the hill for the same purpose, York and Selena finally managed to ride all the way to the bottom.

"There may be something to be said for fun and games in the snow," York observed teasingly as they got back onto the sled for another ride. He wrapped his arms around her, pulling her intimately against his body and cradling her between his legs.

"You're interfering with my steering," Selena protested, thrilling to the embrace as she sat in front of him on the little vehicle.

"Nonsense. I'm just making sure I don't fall overboard." He hugged her tighter and found an uncovered place behind her ear to drop a tantalizing little kiss.

"York! The kids!"

"It'll give them something to look forward to when they grow up."

Selena had never spent a happier afternoon. The laughter and growing sense of intimacy on several levels left her tingling and deliciously content with life. It was almost dusk before York picked up the sled in one hand, clasped Selena's fingers in the other, and headed back to the lodge for hot, spiced wine and a good dinner.

The promised storm arrived at just about the same time. York and Selena lounged near the blazing hearth of the lodge, watching the snow falling through the large windows while they sipped an after-dinner cognac.

"Something tells me this scene would look even more delightful if viewed through the windows of the Fletchers' apartment," York murmured softly, setting down the nearly empty snifter and reaching for Selena's hand.

"Do you think so?" she tried to retort lightly, conscious of a sudden wave of shyness at the look in his eyes. "Same snow, after all . . ."

"Trust me," he whispered. "It'll look a lot different."

"York? Everything's happening rather . . . rather quickly, isn't it?" she began a little earnestly as he pulled her gently to her feet and guided her toward the door.

"Do you want to slow everything down?" he asked with a hint of challenge.

"No," admitted Selena with total honesty.

He tugged her close to his side, chaining her there with an arm around her shoulders. "Like I said a minute ago, trust me."

The whipping snow greeted them as they found the path back to the condominium, and in mild annoyance York removed his glasses and shoved them inside his new fleece-lined suede jacket. He hurried them forward.

"Stay here for a moment, sweetheart," he ordered as they reached the hallway. "I'll be right back."

Selena turned in surprise. "Where are you going?"

"I want to get some things out of the car."

She waited obediently as his long stride carried him temporarily out of sight behind the building. When he reappeared a few minutes later, he was carrying a black leather briefcase.

"Not all of us can afford two whole weeks off from work on such short notice," he told her in response to her inquiringly raised brow. "Like it or not, I'd better spend a couple of hours going over some papers in the morning."

Selena stifled the pang of disappointment. She was being totally unreasonable expecting him to devote the full two weeks to her. After all, he certainly hadn't had time to put his business affairs in order before leaving Pasadena.

"In the morning?" she queried. "Not tonight?"

He swept her down the hall. "Definitely not tonight," he drawled throatily. "Tonight I'm going to show you how different the snow looks from in front of our own fireplace!"

A few minutes later, curled into the corner of the couch, Selena sat watching as York built a fire. His dark hair caught the light of the flames as they sprang to life. Arm resting on one bent knee as he crouched in front of the hearth, he watched to make certain the kindling had caught and then rose with easy masculine grace and crossed the room to where Selena waited.

"You do that pretty well for a Southern Californian who probably doesn't get much practice," she praised. She knew she was saying the words more for something to say than anything else. In the intimacy of the apartment her excitement and awareness of him were overpoweringly strong. It was an effort to maintain a casual, easy manner.

He sank down beside her on the couch and drew her close, stretching his legs out comfortably toward the flames. "Wait until you see me at a barbecue fire. This is a cinch compared to that!"

Selena smiled tremulously, leaning her head against his shoulder. "I can't wait."

"You'll get plenty of opportunity to admire my talents," he promised, beginning to nuzzle the exquisitely sensitive line of her throat. When Selena shivered and nestled closer, he sighed in evident satisfaction and removed his glasses.

"Such a convenience having contacts," he murmured, nibbling her earlobe.

"I'm not so sure about that. What about the awkward little moment last night when I had to excuse myself to go into the bath and take them out before going to sleep?"

"A moment of shared intimacy."

"Uh huh. Some sharing. You had fallen asleep by the time I got back to bed!" She turned her face toward his chest. Slowly, with a sense of anticipation, she unbuttoned his shirt far enough to enable herself to find the first curling tendrils of hair on his chest.

"I woke up again later, as I recall," he pointed out virtuously. His hand slid along her thigh, over the shape of her hip, and up to a spot just beneath the weight of her breast.

"Yes, you did." He'd reached for her in the darkness, making her his once more with a silent, purposeful intensity.

"Selena?" His voice was thickening as she threaded her fingertips through the dark hair.

"Hmmm?"

"You're mine now. You know that, don't you, darling?"

She moved a little restlessly against him. "Are you mine?" she finally countered.

"Cautious little thing, aren't you?" And then the humor faded completely as he scooped her up and set her on the rug at his feet. An instant later he was beside her, unfastening the buttons of her white shirt. "I'm yours, sweetheart. There. Now you've wrung the words out of me, I'm going to wring them out of you!"

His hand slipped inside the opening of her shirt, closing possessively over a breast. Selena moaned deeply as his mouth took hers in a searing kiss that gave off more warmth than the fire on the hearth.

The flames seemed to lick over her body as York undressed her and Selena twisted in rising need. He tugged off his own clothes impatiently and knelt beside her on the rug.

Slowly, deliberately, passionately, he ran his hands over her, stroking her until she was nearly out of her mind with aching desire.

"Tell me, Selena," he commanded hoarsely as she reached blindly for him, trying to pull him to her. "Tell me you're mine!"

And Selena, who would have said anything to please him, let alone the truth, whispered the words he was determined to hear.

"Yes, York. I'm yours. Please ... please ..."

The plea was cut off with shocking suddenness as he moved, parting her thighs with his knee and coming to her with fierce demand. It was a demand she met with an equally vital one of her own. Then the incoherent words of passion took over and Selena was locked with York in an embrace that sealed out the rest of the universe. The fire on the hearth flared higher.

It was hours later that Selena awoke alone in her bed. Blinking in the darkness, she stretched out a toe, seeking contact with York's hard frame. He had carried her into the bedroom a long time ago and they had slept, exhausted, in each other's arms.

When her questing toe found the bed empty, Selena stirred and sat up, automatically holding the sheet to her chin although it quickly became evident there was no one in the room to see her nakedness. Especially not York, who would have found her modesty amusing.

"York?"

She listened intently to hear him moving about in the bath. There was no sound from the adjoining room, however. Yawning sleepily, Selena slid to the edge of the rumpled bed. Perhaps he'd gone out to the kitchen for a glass of water.

Fumbling for the light-plum-and-gold-patterned kimono she had brought along to use as a robe, Selena padded out of the bedroom and into the short hall. At the opposite end a light burned. Still blinking against the influence of sleep, Selena went toward it.

"What in the world . . . !"

She stopped short at the sight of York seated at the teak dining room table, various papers from his briefcase spread out across its surface. Selena glanced toward the kitchen clock but couldn't quite make out the numbers without her contacts. She didn't have to see it, though, to realize it was still the middle of the night. Darkness bathed the slopes outside the window.

"No need to get up quite this early, honey," York said smoothly, turning in his chair at her exclamation. He was barefoot, wearing his jeans and an unbuttoned shirt that exposed the tanned contours of his chest. His black hair was tousled but he looked wide awake behind the lenses of his glasses.

"Do you normally? Get up this early, I mean?" she retorted, moving silently forward across the carpet. She stifled another yawn and came to a halt beside his chair.

He put an arm around her waist and kissed the rounded shape of her breast beneath the satiny kimono. "Don't worry. Normally I keep reasonable hours. There were a couple of things I was thinking about after you went to sleep on me, though, and I..."

"I didn't go to sleep on you!"

"After you decided to rest your eyes for a while," he amended complacently. "At any rate, I decided to get up and work on them."

"What kinds of things?" she asked interestedly, bending forward to peer at the papers on the table.

"Business," he told her a little shortly and gathered up several sheets that were covered with figures. He stacked them together and put them in a pile just slightly out of her reach.

Instantly Selena experienced a flush of guilt. "Am I making life very difficult for you by asking you to stay here in Utah?"

"You're making life very exciting for me here in Utah." He grinned wolfishly, putting his other hand around her waist and pulling her down into his lap. "Don't worry about the business end of things. I can manage." He bent his head and touched the tip of his tongue to the corner of her mouth.

"You don't have to get up in the middle of the night to do this," she said. "I'm not that demanding! I'll let you have some time off from sledding during the day to keep up with your work!"

He chuckled, and moved his hand to the vee of the sashed kimono. He edged one finger just inside and slid it down to the top of her breast. "On the contrary, my dear, you are a very demanding woman! But I always knew you would be and I wouldn't want it any other way."

She blushed and nestled closer. "What do you mean you always knew I would be demanding?" she muttered a little crossly. "We hardly knew each other until you showed up here in Utah!"

"You know that isn't true," he returned, his voice suddenly heavy with meaning. "You and I knew a lot about each other right from the first. If you hadn't been feeling that misplaced loyalty toward Anderson, you wouldn't have shied away from me so often."

"It wasn't that," she began uncertainly. "You ... you made me nervous, York. Wary."

"Are you still afraid of me?"

"I was never afraid of you!" she declared staunchly.

"Prove it!" he drawled, getting to his feet with her in his arms and starting back toward the bedroom.

She laughed up at him, putting her arms comfortably around his neck. "Okay. But where did you get this idea that I'm the kind of woman who responds to dares?"

"I told you, I know you," he repeated unperturbed.

The next time Selena drifted back to awareness it was morning. She knew without any toe exploration this time that York still slept by her side. The weight of one of his ankles trapped hers as if he could bind her to him even in sleep. She smiled contentedly to herself. York hadn't gone back to work a second time last night!

Slowly, carefully, she eased her foot out from under his and climbed lightly out of bed, intent on the little domestic surprise of fixing his breakfast. They had picked up some groceries the day before and Selena knew she had the makings for buckwheat cakes and strong coffee. A perfect snow country breakfast. What was it about this cold air that gave one such an appetite? Or were there other factors involved? she added with a wryly affectionate glance back at the bed as she slipped on the kimono.

She left York's lean, strong body sprawled in sleep and headed first for the bathroom to insert her contact lenses and then to the kitchen, where she plugged in the coffeemaker that had come with the fully equipped vacation apartment. The plum and gold kimono floated gracefully about her ankles as she performed the little chore.

Yawning deliciously, she started back toward the bath. She would shower first and then mix up the buckwheat batter. It was the sight of York's business papers still stacked neatly to one side of the dining room table that halted her progress.

In that moment she could not have said exactly what drew her to the table. It wasn't merely curiosity or any impulse as base as a simple desire to pry. She was motivated by something else altogether, perhaps the too-familiar flicker of intuition.

Almost against her will she found herself reaching out to lift the first page of figures from the pile. At first the numbers and short financial statements made no sense and she started to toss down the sheet in her hand. What business was this of hers?

Then the words "Anderson & Company" in the introductory paragraph on the next page caught her eye. The flicker of intuition that had drawn her to the table leaped into full-fledged premonition. A little unsteadily Selena reached for the next sheet in the stack of papers. She sank slowly into a chair and began to read carefully.

It was, she told herself with a fatalistic, unnatural calm, her own misfortune that her interest in the world of business gave her the background to take an educated guess at what she was reading. She should have stuck to art and not tried to mix the two fields.

The stylized clock on the kitchen wall silently recorded the passing time. The automatic drip coffeemaker finished its task of making coffee and switched to a warming function. Selena ignored them both and continued to read.

She was thoroughly lost in the intricate financial data spread out in front of her, and the tension within her grew with every page she took from the stack.

It grew, tautening every fiber of her body until it was shattered abruptly by the sound of York's sardonic voice behind her.

"How nice to know you're the kind of woman who takes a personal interest in her lover's work."

Selena's head came up with a snap as she spun around in her chair to find him lounging at the entrance to the living room. He was wearing only the low-slung jeans, and the sleek, half-naked power of him seemed to reach across the room to menace her. A thoroughly dangerous man. How could she have forgotten that for even one moment?

He lounged in the doorway the way a predator lounges, and the air between the two of them fairly crackled with the force of the danger. Selena's knuckles whitened as she clutched the arm of her chair. Her hazel eyes were wide and full of the accusations she was about to make. There was pain behind the accusations but she was determined to keep it hidden at all costs. He would not have that satisfaction! It was imperative to deny him at least that much.

"You meant it, didn't you?" she got out huskily. "Literally."

He didn't move. "Meant what?" One black brow rose in a quelling expression.

"You're going to crush Anderson & Company. You're not just out to win the current contract you're both planning to bid for. You're out to ruin Richard's firm completely."

"I told you that the night of the art society reception," he reminded her with a small, too-casual shrug.

"I thought . . . I thought you were bluffing or boasting. I didn't think you could really do it," admitted Selena quietly.

"I never bluff."

It was the chill, even certainty that shook her. "I was right about you from the beginning, wasn't I?" she whispered. "You're a very dangerous man."

"Did you think I had changed all my plans for Anderson & Company simply because I met you?" he asked with a coolness that rasped her nerves.

"No." She shook her head as if a little dazed. "The truth is, I didn't really think at all for a while. If I had I never would have found myself in this situation, would I?" The bitterness seeped into her words in spite of her attempt to avoid any show of emotion.

The watchful gray-green eyes narrowed assessingly. With any other man Selena would have sworn she detected an element of wariness.

"What happened between you and me would have occurred regardless of outside circumstances," he told her roughly. "My war with Anderson & Company is completely independent of us. Do you understand, Selena? It doesn't affect you and me."

"War," she repeated incredulously. "That's what it is, isn't it?" She waved a hand in disdainful dismissal of the papers on the table. "All these facts and figures. All this debt structure analysis, cash flow details, income per share information. You don't need this kind of data simply to make a competitive bid for an engineering project. This is the kind of information someone would gather if he were interested in taking over another company by force. And you can do it, can't you? You've found the weaknesses in Anderson & Company. You're going to go for the throat.''

''It has nothing to do with you and me, Selena!'' he reiterated flatly.

''How can you stand there and lie to me like that? It has everything to do with you and me! I was just a pawn, wasn't I? A useful bit of psychological warfare. Oh, yes, I'm fully aware that psychological tactics are as important in an unfriendly takeover attempt as financial maneuvers. I read *The Wall Street Journal!*''

''Selena!'' he grated.

''During the past two days I let you convince me that I had somehow misjudged you. I thought both of us had been caught up in something much more important than business. But now that I've seen how thoroughly you mean to ruin Richard, I realized there couldn't have been room for anything else in your head except plans for the war in which you're involved. You wanted to take me away from Richard because of the psychological advantage it would provide. It was merely a guerilla tactic, wasn't it? What are you going to do when we return to Pasadena? Spread the word around that you've bedded Anderson's girlfriend?''

"Stop it, Selena!" The command was a harsh sound as York straightened from his lounging position in the doorway and started toward her.

Selena instinctively got to her feet as if preparing to meet a physical assault. Indeed, she felt very much like a trapped gazelle facing a stalking hunting cat. But she had one distinct advantage over a gazelle. She could rail at her attacker, defy him, accuse him. For all the good it would do!

"I must have lost my head during the past couple of days. Perhaps I let myself be hypnotized. I don't know. Whatever made me think I had been wrong about you? You're the same man you were when I first met you. Nothing has changed. Winning is all that concerns you, and winning to you means crushing your opponent completely. No gentlemen's rules for you. My God! Is the fact that you lost that one contract to Anderson & Company a few months ago so damaging to your ego that you have to not only win the next one but destroy Richard in the process?''

York was almost upon her and Selena braced herself with her hands behind her back, gripping the edge of the table. Chin tilted defiantly, she faced him with all the accusing scorn she could summon. She would not let him see how well he had managed to trample her in the process of conducting his war games. Unexpectedly he halted two paces away and pinned her with hard, aggressive eyes.

"For the last time, Selena, what's going on between myself and Anderson does not affect you and me. For your information the man's got coming to him everything he's going to get!"

"Because his firm was sharp enough to win that last bidding competition?" she shot back disbelievingly. "That was merely business and you know it!"

"He cheated."

"Oh, come on, York . . . !"

"You don't believe me?"

"Hardly!"

"It's the truth, damn it, and I'm not going to stand here defending myself to you!" York suddenly blazed, losing a portion of the cold, arrogant control that had cloaked his anger. "I will outline the story for you once and once only. Anderson & Company has severe internal problems. I told you the man doesn't have his father's talents. The firm needed to win that last engineering contract or face a huge deficit this year. A deficit that might very well have cost Richard his position as chief executive officer. The board would have had to do something to appease the stockholders. He's only in that role because of the loyalty the company still feels toward his father. In an effort to maintain his position your ex-boyfriend resorted to a little corporate espionage against his prime competitor, Sutherland, Inc. By the time I discovered what had happened it was too late. Anderson had the contract. But he's going to pay for it, Selena. I made that vow months ago and I intend to keep it! I'll bring down his entire house of cards!''

"You can't do that!" Selena gasped, appalled at the vengeance in his words.

"Why not?" York asked with deadly simplicity.

"You don't understand. If you succeed in destroying Richard's firm and his position in it, you would destroy him personally. And not only him, but his family, their standing in the community—"

"Interestingly enough, I won't be destroying his wife," York interrupted ruthlessly. "Remember her? The woman he wasn't about to leave for your sake? It won't hurt her, Selena, because she's the one with the money. It's been her money that has kept the Anderson fortunes afloat for the past five years. That's why Richard married her and that's why he won't divorce her. It was a classic marriage of convenience. Her money for his status and an entrée into the old-money crowd. She'll turn a blind eye toward most things, such as her husband's little affairs, but she sure as hell won't ignore his loss of status. She'll take her money and leave him flat.''

"You won't get anywhere ramming the facts about Richard's marriage down my throat! And that's what you're trying to do, isn't it? Convince me to support you by reminding me that Richard tried to use me?''

"You were furious at having been misled by him. Don't deny it!''

"Yes, I'll admit that. But I put a stop to it. I told him what I thought of him and I got myself out of the situation.''

"Was that enough for you?" York baited. "Wouldn't you have liked a little more in the way of revenge? Come on, Selena, you're human enough for that and you've got a temper.''

"Perhaps I've already taken my revenge against Richard,'' Selena tossed back, goaded. "Perhaps that's the real reason I let you seduce me. What better revenge could a woman have against a man than to go to bed with his sworn enemy?''

"No!" he thundered, closing the short gap between them with one pouncing step. He caught her by her arms, his fingers digging into her flesh through the light fabric of the wide kimono sleeves. His face was a savage and alien terrain as even more of his control slipped. "That wasn't the reason you gave yourself to me! Don't lie to me like that!"

Selena licked nervously dry lips. It had been a spur-of-the-moment act of retaliation and self-defense to taunt him with such an explanation for her surrender. She was startled by the extent of his reaction.

"What do you care about my reasons for letting you seduce me? You got what you wanted out of the situation—a weapon to use against Richard. Why deny me my own personal revenge? You just got through saying I must have wanted some!"

"Damn it, woman . . . !"

"Stop swearing at me!"

"You're right, I shouldn't be swearing at you," he agreed between clenched teeth. "I should be beating the truth out of you. Nothing has changed, Selena Caldwell. The situation between us is the same as it was last night before you began snooping through my business papers."

"No, York, it isn't," Selena managed with a steadiness that surprised her. "It's true, you are the same man you were all along, but it has been forcibly driven home to me that I made a tremendous error in judgment. I refuse to become involved with a man so bent on winning at any cost that he'll use anyone he can to achieve this goal."

"I didn't use you!"

"Even if I could believe that, it wouldn't alter the fact that you're the kind of man who would bring down an entire family for the sake of revenge. I have no sympathy for Richard, God knows, after what he did to me, and you have every right to ace him out of this upcoming contract if what you tell me is the truth about the way he cheated. But that should be the end of it. If he's as poor a businessman as you say, let him ruin himself. Deliberately acting to bring about the process will make you as bad as he is!"

"You don't understand," York gritted. "No one gets away with cheating me. He deserves to lose everything. I don't let anyone step on me, Selena. That's not how a man survives in this world."

She stared up at him mutely, aware of his punishing grip on her arm and the utter determination in his voice. What had happened to the man she had laughed and loved with during the past two days? Had he only been an illusion? A creation of her own mind brought about by a desire to justify her surrender to the compelling fascination York held for her? How could she have been so stupid?

"It's obvious I can't stop you, York," she finally said bleakly. "But I don't have to help you any more than I already have. Go back to your battle and leave me alone." Her mouth twisted wryly as she added, "I'd say something trite like 'may the best man win' but it would be a little hypocritical, wouldn't it? Right now neither one of you qualifies as the 'best.' In any event, judging by what I've seen in those papers, you'll probably be the victor. When it comes to carrying out your vengeance, you appear to do your homework very thoroughly. The sign of a good battle commander, I'm sure. Goodbye, York."

"You're not leaving, Selena," he muttered, anchoring her with manacles of steel around her arms. "Not until we've sorted this out."

"There's nothing left to sort out. I know exactly what you're after and I don't intend to become any more involved than I already have. Let me go, York. Now. Face it," she told him savagely, "this is one small skirmish you can't win. You can't hold me prisoner here and you know it. But look at it this way, you don't need me anymore so why go to the bother of trying to defeat me in this little matter? After having been used by both Richard and yourself, surely I deserve to be hors de combat!"

For a moment she thought she had lost the small gambit and that he really would find a way to keep her prisoner. Then the slitted green eyes became assessing once more as York clearly regained control of his frustrated anger. To Selena's barely concealed astonishment, he released her, stepping back a single pace.

"Where will you go?" he demanded tightly. "Back to Pasadena?"

"Where else?" She shrugged, trying to appear calm and disdainfully unconcerned. She deliberately circled him, heading toward the bedroom. Without a backward glance she made herself walk, not run, to the safety of the other room.

Once out of sight, she gave in to despairing panic, whirling to lock the door behind her. Then, taking several deep breaths to choke back the sobs that were threatening to well up in her throat, she flung herself into the adjoining bath and turned on the shower with a violent gesture.

It took more courage than she could have imagined to reenter the living room forty-five minutes later, her small bag packed and clutched in her left hand. She was wearing her jeans and a white pleated shirt with a defiant splash of brilliant persimmon in a scarf that circled her throat. She paused for a moment, her eyes instantly clashing with those of the man who waited for her.

York was still wearing only his jeans and hadn't bothered to comb the tangle of his ebony hair. A cup of coffee beside him on the dining room table, he sat with masculine casualness in the chair she had occupied earlier. The damning papers were still spread out where Selena had left them. What did a woman say at a time like this? she wondered almost hysterically. Perhaps everything that needed to be said had already been uttered.

Her mouth firming, Selena started toward the door, aware of the gaze that followed her. She could virtually feel the hard force of his will reaching out to stop her but she fought it with every ounce of her being. She must not give in to him, not this time. This man knew only winning and losing, and she would not lose to him a second time.

Mercifully the doorknob was finally in the grasp of her fingers. She twisted, pulling it toward her, half expecting the jaguar in the chair behind her to leap at the last minute and drag her back to his lair. The feeling of danger radiating across the room was a tangible force. An irresistible force, she reminded herself wretchedly. That was how her imagination had characterized York Sutherland. She certainly hadn't turned out to be an immovable object!

The awesome silence continued until she had actually made it into the hallway outside the apartment and then York finally spoke, his deliberate, too-quiet words sending a shiver down her spine.

"This isn't the end of it, Selena, and you know it. You can run once more but I'll be right behind you. You can't escape."

Six

The damnable part was that she believed him! Even as she drove the twenty miles of interstate freeway out of the mountains and back to Salt Lake City, Selena found herself glancing occasionally into the rearview mirror looking for the rental car he had driven up to the lodge. Boarding the plane bound for Los Angeles International, she found herself looking back over her shoulder. York Sutherland wasn't the type of man who made idle threats. She had to face the fact that he meant what he'd said; he would follow her. She didn't relax until the 737 was taxiing down the runway.

But the reprieve was only temporary. York might very well be on the next plane, and what was she going to do when she found him at her front door? Because under all the hurt and anger Selena knew she still loved the man.

It was altogether different this time, she mused sadly as she took advantage of the airline's offer of a drink. When she'd discovered Richard's treachery, she had been furious but she hadn't felt this crushing unhappiness. Her pride had been hurt and she'd had every reason for the anger, but never for a moment had she thought her heart was any more than superficially involved. This time the pain went deeper than she could have believed possible. Deeper in some strange way even than it had the day she finally acknowledged that her marriage had been a mistake.

What had York Sutherland done to her in the few short weeks she had known him that enabled him to have such an effect on her? She had known from the first that he wasn't right for her, known he was dangerous; yet when he'd tracked her down at the lodge and confronted her with his need and desire, she had grasped at the illusion of a changed man...

A changed man, she repeated over and over again. Selena was still repeating the phrase even as she finally turned the key in her Pasadena apartment and walked into the familiar, eclectic atmosphere. What did it take to really change an irresistible force?

It took an immovable object, she reminded herself bitterly. She certainly hadn't qualified as that. One would have thought that at her age she would have had the common sense to realize she had no business becoming involved with a man like York Sutherland. But how could she have resisted the irresistible force? she comforted herself wryly as she slowly unpacked and settled down after the thwarted vacation.

What would become of the driving force that was Sutherland? Selena poured herself a glass of Chablis and wandered out into her white living room. Sinking into the sofa, she sipped the drink and stared sightlessly at the incredible swirl of paint that decorated a canvas on the opposite wall. It wasn't a bad painting, Selena thought idly, just a misunderstood painting. Perhaps someday the artist would learn to make his work more accessible. It was a lot more likely that the artist would learn from his mistakes than that York would learn from his defeats. Because York didn't tolerate defeats very well!

Perhaps that's what it would take to jolt him into a less adversarial approach to life, Selena thought fleetingly: a defeat that was serious enough to make him change his priorities. It was a cinch that as long as the man kept winning, he wasn't going to change.

Selena swirled the wine in her glass and ruthlessly told herself that she didn't have the power to effect such a drastic change in York Sutherland. Probably no woman had that much power.

But he wanted her, she reminded herself wonderingly. It was true that she had also been useful to him, but was it possible that had only been a coincidence? Had he been telling the truth when he'd claimed that his desire for her had nothing to do with his plans for Anderson & Company?

Biting her lip in self-inflicted punishment at her own stupidity, Selena tried to put the thought aside. She was not going to tell herself fairy tales at this stage!

But she knew, even as she told herself not to give in to the desire to weave a fantasy around York Sutherland, that she loved him and that sooner or later she would once more find him at her door. Her fingers tightened in anguish on the stem of the glass. What was she going to do when that moment arrived?

By the time she undressed and slid beneath the covers of her all-white bed, Selena was no closer to a solution. As she reached out to turn off a monstrosity of a lamp that had been given to her by a local craftsman, she found herself wondering at the fact that the evening had passed in peace. She had no doubt that York would put in an appearance eventually, but she wasn't sure her nerves were going to take very well to a game of cat-and-mouse in the meantime.

She awoke the next morning, after a fitful night, with a groggy sense of disorientation. The first thing that struck her was that she didn't have to go to work that day. In fact, it would only cause a lot of questions if she did. But she certainly wasn't going to spend the day hanging around her apartment waiting for the axe to fall!

What she needed was an antidote to the overdose of business to which she'd been subjected lately. Selena considered her options over her morning coffee and then headed for Pasadena's Norton Simon Museum.

There, amid a remarkable collection that ranged from the early Renaissance to the twentieth century, Selena began to relax. She strolled through the sculpture garden and eventually found herself in the portion of the gallery she loved best, the section housing the work of the French impressionists. She was examining with pleasure a painting by Monet when a familiar voice called her name.

"Selena! What are you doing here? Taking a day off work?" The blue-eyed, bearded man in his mid-thirties who was strolling toward her seemed genuinely pleased to see her. He was dressed in a paint-stained pair of jeans and a blue work shirt and he carried a sketch pad under one arm.

"Hello, Chris. Soaking up a little technique?" She smiled, thrusting her hands into the back pockets of her own jeans.

"Never hurts." He chuckled good-naturedly. "I'm never too proud to steal what I can from those who have gone before me!"

"Which is probably one of the reasons you're among the few successful artists I know," returned Selena. "You have the sense not to waste time re-inventing the wheel. Studying the impressionists today?"

"Ummm. How about you?"

"Just browsing. I have a few days off and I needed to get away from the business side of things." She shrugged.

"You walk a fine line at times, don't you?" He nodded with the understanding of an old friend. "Do you ever regret not giving all your energy to creating instead of selling art materials?"

She shook her head thoughtfully. "No. I still dabble occasionally but it would never have been more than a hobby for me, Chris. I'm too easily sidetracked by my interest in the world of business. It's quite fascinating, you know, making a business successful."

"Fascinating for you, perhaps," he told her with a wry twist of his mouth. "Personally, I hate that end of things."

"Without that end of things you wouldn't have access to all the supplies you need for your work!" she reminded him lightly. "You'd still be grinding your own paints and worrying about whether or not they would last more than a few months on the canvas! It's modern business that has brought you the technology of good, reliable materials!"

He threw up one palm laughingly. "Enough! I surrender! Believe me, I'm grateful there are people like you out there in the world. I guess I just don't see how you can skate back and forth between the two worlds. It's obvious you love art..."

"And I love my work," she concluded firmly. "Not all of us are as singlemindedly dedicated as you are."

"Or perhaps some of us are able to live in two worlds at the same time," he suggested gently.

"Without the driving willpower to make a thorough-going success in either world," she finished dryly.

Chris frowned. "What's that supposed to mean?"

Selena moved one shoulder in a dismissing motion. "It's hard to explain, Chris. It has nothing to do with the fact that you'd starve for your art and I know someone who will stop at nothing to build a business empire. Neither of you would allow anything else to get in the way of achieving your goals."

"Please!" he protested. "I'd just as soon not be compared to some business tycoon!"

"But maybe there is something in common between the two of you," Selena continued thoughtfully, her mind picking up the pieces left behind after her disastrous encounter with York Sutherland and examining them from a new angle. She eyed her friend curiously. "Tell me something, Chris. What would it take to deflect you from finishing a painting you'd started?"

He cocked his head to one side, sensing the seriousness of the strange question. "It's hard to say, Selena. Perhaps the inspiration for another painting that suddenly became more urgent than the one I was working on. Or I might stop work on a project if I realized it wasn't going to turn out the way I had planned. I wouldn't waste time pursuing it, I suppose," he said slowly. "What's all this about, Selena?"

"I'm not sure, Chris. Just trying to understand the inner workings of the driven personality, I guess," she told him with a forced smile. "Come on, let's go take a look at the Degas exhibit downstairs."

To her relief Chris was kind enough to let the subject drop, and they soon became enmeshed in a vigorous discussion of the art they were viewing. Running into him, she realized, had been a blessing. He was a friend, pure and simple. The point when the two of them might have found something more together had come and gone a long time ago. They would never be right for each other that way and they had both quietly acknowledged it. But everyone needed friends.

The day passed quickly, and when Chris invited her to join him at a small espresso bar tucked away in an alley near downtown, Selena readily accepted. She didn't want to admit that the temptation to avoid going home as long as possible was a strong one.

Eventually, however, the time came, and it wasn't the art she had viewed that day nor the interesting conversation with friends in the espresso bar that occupied Selena's mind on the drive home. It was Chris's comment when she had asked him what it would take to keep him from finishing a painting. "... If I realized it wasn't going to turn out the way I had planned ..."

York Sutherland was a hard-headed business-man, driven by a passion that might not be all that different from Chris Worthington's. If he realized that his goal of crushing Anderson & Company wasn't going to turn out the way he had planned, could he be deflected from it? Could he be forced to recognize other priorities in life?

"My God, Selena," she whispered to herself as she parked her red Toyota in the underground parking garage, "what the devil do you think you're playing at? Sutherland could tear you to pieces if you tried to stop him!"

It all hinged, she realized, on how badly he wanted her and on who could outbluff whom. She closed her eyes at the thought of trying to bluff York Sutherland.

Time was running out. Soon she would be facing the man, and if she didn't have some tac-tics ready and waiting to use against him, she would be helpless to deal with his newest as-sault. It wasn't just his desire he would want to satisfy this time; he would be angry, too. A lethal combination.

It would be easier if she knew exactly when he would choose to reappear in her life, though, she thought ruefully as she entered her apartment with a sigh of relief at finding it empty. She was under no illusion about the present skirmish. York would let her worry and fret about his next appearance. Good tactics, she thought disgustedly.

Selena had begun to think she was going to get through another evening without having to deal with the predator in her life when the doorbell chimed with such authority that her intuition leaped to the inevitable conclusion. Time had run out.

It took an astonishing amount of nerve to open the door. She knew who would be standing on the other side as surely as if he'd already announced himself. Desperately Selena tried to put her own poor strategy in order as she opened the door and met York's hooded, assessing gaze.

"Had enough time to get over the tantrum?" he asked laconically. He stood aggressively across the threshold from her, his feet slightly apart and braced in a challenging stance. The close-fitting jeans looked like the same ones in which she had last seen him. He wore them with a casual, open-throated white shirt and the leather jacket he'd taken to Utah. It was obvious that York hadn't spent the day in the office. That seemed odd. But, then, she really didn't know where he lived. Perhaps he'd gone home to change?

"Taking the offense right from the start, I see," Selena managed coolly, making no attempt to block his entrance into the apartment. There would have been no point and they both knew it. "A question nicely calculated to put me on the defensive. If I say yes, I admit I was merely indulging a tantrum, if I say no, I admit the same thing."

"So you'll probably choose to skirt the issue," he concluded with a nod, striding boldly into her apartment.

"I shall ignore the question because it is totally irrelevant. I did not stage a tantrum." She closed the door with a small slam and turned to watch as he shrugged out of his jacket and sprawled on her sofa.

"You haven't tried to throw me out yet," he drawled. "I suppose that's a good sign."

"If I asked you to leave, would you go?"

"No."

Selena stepped away from the door. "If you won't go willingly, there's not much point in my trying to toss you out on your ear, is there? You're bigger than I am."

He eyed her thoughtfully. "If it were a physical possibility, would you do it?"

"A moot point, isn't it?" she shot back sardonically. "You'll never know. Why don't you tell me what you're hoping to accomplish by showing up on my doorstep this evening? Shouldn't you be working late in your office, preparing your revenge against Richard?" she taunted, sitting down across from him.

"I haven't been in the office at all today. I just got back from Utah," York said calmly.

"Utah! Why did you stay up there?" The remark had taken her by surprise. She'd assumed he'd flown out of Salt Lake City immediately behind her.

"I needed to do some thinking," he admitted quietly. "And I needed to give you some time to do the same. If I'd come back from Utah yesterday, I wouldn't have been able to prevent myself from coming over here last night. I figured we both needed the time."

"Very generous of you," she murmured dryly. "Are you sure you weren't delaying your arrival in an attempt to keep me on edge?"

"Were you on edge?" he countered softly, eyes taking on a partially concealed gleam almost at once. The hunter in him, Selena thought distantly. He couldn't quite hide it.

"As a matter of fact, I spent the time exactly as you suggest I should have spent it. Thinking." She narrowed her gaze and tried for a casual pose in the chair she was occupying. The casualness was only skin-deep, for with those words she had taken the first step in her own private war. A frisson comprised of both recklessness and fear flashed along her nerve endings as the audacious scheme that had been in the back of her mind slowly crystalized in her thoughts.

As if he sensed the impending firefight, York's expression suddenly became very watchful as he studied Selena's slender figure curled in the chair. "You have, I take it, come to a few conclusions?"

"Yes."

"Preparing to run again, Selena?" he baited softly.

"No, York, I'm not running away from you anymore," she told him firmly, her pulses beginning to race with the nervous dread in her system.

"Dare I hope you've come to your senses and realized that my plans for Anderson & Company are entirely separate from my plans for us?"

"Oh, no, York," she said in her gentlest accents. "The two sets of plans are very closely intertwined. You're going to have to make a choice, you see. For what is probably the first time in your life, you're going to find out you can't always have your cake and eat it, too."

He swore half under his breath, something short and succinct. His eyes never left hers although she was at a loss to tell what he was thinking behind the shield of his glasses. "Let me guess," he grated icily. "You're about to tell me I can't have you and my revenge, too, right? I'll save you time and trouble and tell you right now, it won't work. I can have you and I think you know that. Whatever else is involved here, one thing's for sure. You're as attracted to me as I am to you and nothing's going to change that."

Selena sat silently, unmoving, while she absorbed the impact of his arrogance.

York sat back more deeply into the corner of the couch, lifting one foot to prop it on the coffee table. "I'm sorry if I pulled the teeth out of your threats before you even had a chance to utter them, honey. But in the long run it won't matter, believe me. I'll convince you that our relationship has nothing to do with Anderson. I'm not using you and eventually you're going to see that for yourself!''

Selena tore her half-hypnotized gaze away and stared out the window. ''Do you know something, York? I'm beginning to believe you.''

She sensed his abrupt relaxation. ''I thought, or rather I hoped, that after you'd had a little time to think, you'd realize that what we had in bed the past couple of nights was at least honest. Selena, you won't regret this, I swear it. I wasn't using you.'' The words came out in the thankful tone of a man who has tensed himself for battle only to have the enemy surrender without a fight.

''I'm glad to hear that, York, but whatever the truth of the matter, it has nothing to do with my... my threats, as you just called them.'' She turned her head back to face him, summoning all the willpower at her disposal to meet the flare of anger that had leaped to life in him. Her fingers clenched into her palm as her hand rested in her lap.

''Don't tell me you're still going to try to keep me out of your bed unless I swear to forget my business with Anderson!'' he gritted warningly. ''I've told you, Selena, it won't work. And if you want proof, then go ahead and make your threats. As soon as the words are out of your mouth, I'll carry you into the bedroom and prove you can't make good on them!''

Shivering under the impact of his promise, Selena got restlessly to her feet and moved away from him to stand in front of the window. "You're jumping to conclusions, York," she told him bravely. "I wouldn't dream of trying to pretend you couldn't seduce me again. I wasn't going to threaten you with something as trite as telling you that you can't share my bed unless you give up your scheme to ruin Richard.''

"Then why are we conducting this little scene, Selena?'' he rasped heavily, running a hand through his black hair in a gesture of weariness and impatience. "What's going through your too-feminine brain?''

"A very businesslike threat, I assure you," she whispered, confronting him with a proudly held chin.

He closed his eyes momentarily. "All right, let's hear it.''

"So you can proceed to demolish it? It's not going to be that easy, York. You see, I know something about the business world and I've been learning something about the personality of someone who's driven the way you seem to be driven.''

"Spare me the psychological analysis!''

"All right, I'll come to the point. I know the bid figure you're going to be using in the current contract competition. I saw it on one of those papers you left on the table that morning."

"So?" He lifted one brow in that intimidating gesture she was getting to know all too well.

"I also know that forewarned is forearmed in the forced-acquisition game. If Anderson & Company learns of your plans to take over the firm before you have a chance to get everything in place, there's a good chance they'll have time to maneuver and find a way out before you can close the trap."

"You're right. You have been reading *The Wall Street Journal*. What's all this leading up to, Selena?" York demanded evenly.

"I'm offering a deal," Selena returned in the same tone. "I won't leak what I know about the bid figures or the takeover plans if you'll scrap the latter."

Heart pounding, her hands in a damp tangle behind her back, Selena waited for his reaction. What had she done? Who was she to take on this prowling hunter at his own game? What had made her think she could intimidate York Sutherland, of all people?

"That's not exactly a deal, Selena," he finally observed in a suspiciously neutral tone. "That sort of thing is usually called blackmail." He didn't move but he didn't need to. Selena could feel the sudden menace in him. She swallowed and found her voice.

"Yes, I guess you could call it that."

He came up off the couch in a surging motion that made her take an automatic step backward even though he didn't close the distance between them. She couldn't read the expression in his eyes but it didn't take her finely tuned intuition to know it didn't bode well. She had tried to cage a panther with very weak bars.

"Does Anderson still mean that much to you?" he charged tightly.

"Richard means nothing to me!"

"Then why are you going to such lengths to protect him? He's not worth it, Selena!"

"It's you I'm protecting," she cried, her voice cracking slightly under the strain.

"Me!" he raged, spinning around to stride toward the kitchen. "Me?" he repeated, utterly astonished. "What the hell do you mean by that? I assure you I can take care of myself!"

"What you're planning is wrong, York. Maybe Richard does deserve to lose everything,

I don't know. I do know that if you deliberately bring about his complete downfall merely to revenge yourself for his cheating on that last contract, you'll be doing as much damage to yourself as you will to him!"

"You're out of your mind," he growled from the kitchen, where she could hear him opening and closing closet doors with ill-concealed fury. Finally he seemed to locate whatever it was he was looking for. When he paced back out into the living room, he was holding her one bottle of scotch and a glass.

He flung himself savagely down onto the sofa and poured the scotch. "You're out of your mind," he repeated a little more softly after downing a man-size swallow. "I won't be any different after I've taken care of Anderson. I'll be the same man I've always been." He trapped her gaze challengingly.

"I realize that," she answered simply. "You'll be the same man you've always been." She drew in a steadying breath. "But you see, York, I want a slightly different man. I want to change you."

"I don't believe this," he muttered incredulously.

"I'm not fool enough to think I could just ask you to give up your plans and have you do it,"

Selena went on carefully. "I'm not fool enough to think I could keep you from seducing me again, if you tried. It would take something far stronger than a woman's pleas to make you give up your project. You have to be shown that the project itself is no longer a viable possibility. It can't be completed as planned. I will disrupt all those plans, York."

Seven

"You're bluffing." York downed a sip of the scotch and the gray-green gaze challenged her confidently. "You'd never do it, Selena, and you know it. It's my business, after all, and you wouldn't dare meddle in it."

"I remember you told me in Utah that I'm the kind of woman who takes dares," she managed grimly, refusing to flinch beneath the force of his aggression. It was becoming clear to her, even as she took her stance, that she had to hold firm if she was to accomplish anything at all. Stopping the irresistible force took an immovable object.

If there was to be any hope for their relationship, she would have to be that object.

"Selena, this isn't a joking matter," he gritted, setting down the glass in his hand rather abruptly. "You know nothing about the kind of business I'm engaged in but you should have the sense to stay out of it. You can't change me, honey," he added gently. "I am what I am."

"People can change, York," she returned steadily.

"For God's sake! What do you want to change me to?" he raged huskily. "A weakling? A man who doesn't stand up for himself in a brutal world? I'm going to make Sutherland, Inc., a name to be reckoned with in the engineering world, Selena. I have to serve notice to all competitors that I'm capable of looking out for myself and that I won't be stomped on by anyone. Bringing Anderson to his knees is an effective way of doing it."

"I can't believe it's necessary to go to such lengths to establish your reputation, York!" Selena countered almost pleadingly. "And if you manage to accomplish your goal, where will that leave you? A little more power hungry? A little more brutal? The next time you think someone has dared to get in your way, what will you do to punish him?"

"The question you should be asking yourself," he retorted coolly, "is what will I do to *her?*"

A tide of red flowed up to Selena's cheeks as she absorbed the implications. She was the one who was now trying to get in his way. What would he do to her? Hastily she tried to shut out the fear. That was exactly the reaction he wanted and she must not give him the satisfaction.

"Are you going to destroy Artistic Endeavors in order to punish me?" she tossed back, knowing she had to take the offensive. "It would be an effective technique. I had planned on buying the place in a few months. I assure you, it would crush me to lose it."

"Oh, hell." York eyed her balefully. "Why am I letting myself get into this kind of ridiculous argument? You know damn well I wouldn't do that to you."

She shrugged. "How do I know that? If you thought your sense of machismo was being trampled by me, you might look for a surefire method of putting me in my place...."

"I can promise you there are other methods of bringing you to hell!" The threat was implicit in every shade of his expression as he took another sip of the scotch. "Damn it, Selena, don't push me like this. You're making me say things I don't mean."

Selena's mouth crooked wryly. "I think you do mean them."

"You don't look exactly terrorized."

"With a man like you it's crucial not to show any fear," she allowed gently.

There was a pause while he digested that. "You think I'm some kind of monster."

"If I thought that, I would never have gone to bed with you." The smile that accompanied that small admission was one of those York had praised: warm and genuine, even if it was a little tremulous.

York blinked owlishly under the spell of it and then asked, "Are you sure about that? I get the feeling you're trying to write your own script for Beauty and the Beast!"

"As I recall, the lady managed to tame the beast," Selena murmured whimsically. Then she immediately wished the words unsaid. York, it seemed, knew his fairy tales.

"Love was the technique she used, not blackmail." There was a shuttered look in his eyes as he taunted her.

Selena drew in her breath, momentarily fearful that he had guessed the depths of her feelings for him. How could she ever hold her ground if he knew the full weakness of her defenses? "I prefer to put my trust in something that has a chance of working!"

"And you think blackmail will work?" he growled derisively.

"I can only hope so."

"Why does changing me matter so much?" he challenged bluntly.

There it was, the inevitable question. What was she going to say now? "You must have a pretty good inkling as to the answer to that one," she told him evenly, not meeting his glance.

"You want me," he said confidently.

"Yes." Selena focused very hard on the street scene outside her window.

"But on your own terms," he concluded.

"Yes." This time the affirmative was a bare thread of sound.

She never heard him leave the couch but something made her turn back toward York very quickly in a defensive, nervous manner that belied her attempt to be coolly manipulative. It was too late; he was upon her. He caught her face roughly between his hands, letting the full weight of his willpower and physical superiority impress itself on her.

"Call it quits, sweetheart," York commanded deeply, his probing gaze burning into her tense features. "Forget about the business side of me, it doesn't affect us now and I'll see to it that it never does."

"You can't say that, York. It does affect us. It colors the whole way you look at life, it has to! I want a man who can have some other priorities in life besides winning at any cost!"

"You want *me!* You just said so!"

"I'm not trying to deny that!"

He shook his head slowly, clearly still half-disbelieving. "You're really determined to try and pull off this blackmail stunt, aren't you? It's hard to comprehend, Selena, it just doesn't seem like you..."

"You haven't had a chance to get to know me all that well yet," she reminded him dryly.

"It would seem," he grated deliberately, "that I do have a couple more things to learn about you. Do you have any idea what you're doing, Selena Caldwell? Are you aware of all the risks involved when you dare the devil in a man?" His fingers moved to tighten warningly on the curve of her shoulders. "There could be hell to pay in the end!"

"Go ahead and make your threats, York, I'm not going to back down!" Even if she was beginning to tremble in reaction to the over-charged atmosphere!

"Damn it, Selena . . . !" He brought his rage under control and a hard gleam sprang alive in his eyes. His fingers dug abruptly into the skin of her shoulders as he pulled her close. "Damn it, woman," he repeated tightly, "if I'm going to let you get away with this, you'd better be prepared to maintain your end of the bargain!"

"It isn't exactly a bargain, York . . ." she began to protest.

"Call it what you like, you're going to find I want my money's worth out of every transaction. You're costing me an entire engineering firm, Selena, not to mention the satisfaction I intended to derive from my plans. You'd better make it worth it!" He moved, scooping her up into his arms before she could even make an attempt at escape.

"York, no! Not like this!" Shocked at what she had unleashed, Selena began to struggle in sudden fear.

"If you're intent on interfering in the business side of my life, you'd better learn the rules of the game, sweetheart," he snarled, striding toward her bedroom. "Take it from me, blackmail's a particularly rough version of play!"

"York, please . . . !" she wailed.

"I'm in no mood to please you tonight. I'm in a mood to take what's mine. And you most definitely are mine, Selena," he continued deliberately. "Whatever else is going on between us, that fact remains indisputable. Did you think you could keep me out of your bed until I had been coerced into changing to your specifications?" he mocked.

"Put me down! I refuse to let you treat me like this." Desperately Selena strained against him, trying to break free. In that moment she didn't even care if he dropped her. Anything to halt the obvious direction of his plans!

"Treat you like what? Like a blackmailing, scheming female who has had the very bad judgment to take on more than she can handle?"

"You don't understand! You're deliberately misunderstanding, in fact. Stop trying to frighten me, York!"

"Am I frightening you?" he asked in taunting surprise as he swung through the doorway into her bedroom. "I'm amazed. Women who play the kind of games you're playing shouldn't allow themselves to be so easily scared!"

"I'm not scared!" Selena flung back, outraged by the accusation. "But you have no right to...mmmmph!"

The angry flow of her retort was muffled as York dropped her callously onto the bed. Frantically she floundered to a sitting position, pushing the hair back out of her alarmed eyes in time to see York shedding his shirt and shoes and glasses with quick, effective movements that did more to heighten her fear than any words could have done. He was going to do it, she thought, astounded. He was going to force himself on her!

Regardless of what she knew about the aggressive side of his nature, Selena had never thought he would actually resort to...

"York, this will be rape," she managed very steadily.

"One good crime deserves another," he jibed savagely.

She wasn't going to be able to talk him out of it, Selena realized incredulously. As if hypnotized for a painful moment, she watched him kick off his shoes. Then his hands went to the buckle of his leather belt.

"No...!"

Galvanized into action by the utter intensity of the seething near-green gaze pinning her to the bed, Selena moved. In a flurry of panic she scrambled to the opposite side of the bed, stumbling awkwardly as she found the carpet with her feet and straightened to run.

She heard the bed give dangerously as he planted one foot in the middle and stepped across it in a springing bound that brought him down almost in reach of her on the other side. Selena didn't look back as she raced for the door.

She had almost reached the hallway when the looped leather belt slipped over her wrist. York had caught her as neatly as if she were a small animal he had roped with a lasso. The jolt as he brought her to a sudden halt whipped Selena around to face him. Enraged, she let the momentum carry her outflung hand in a sweeping arc that landed against his cheek in a fierce crack.

"Damn you, York Sutherland, don't you dare do this to me!"

He ignored her outburst, using the belt to draw her inevitably closer to him. Selena swallowed as she saw the way the side of his cheek was turning a vivid red.

"Why are you trying to run from me, Selena?" he grated between set teeth. "We seem to have a deal, you and I. Why aren't you willing to carry out your end?" His fingers closed like twin vises on each of her wrists, holding her captive in front of him.

"I won't let you do this to me," she whispered violently.

"You said you wanted me," he reminded her cruelly.

"Not like this!"

"What did you expect? That I'd be sweet, docile, and charming after hearing your grand scheme?"

She ground her teeth in frustration and fear. How had she expected him to react? she asked herself unhappily. The truth was, she hadn't thought it all through that far. What a mess. A frightening, overwhelming mess. The only thing Selena knew for certain was that she must not back down. Every scrap of her intuition was fairly screaming that advice.

"I expected you'd probably be a bit upset," she began grimly.

"A bit upset!" he echoed in disbelief, dark brows climbing.

"But I never thought you'd resort to violence. I'm only doing it for your sake, York. For both our sakes," she added pleadingly.

"You're crazy," he stated flatly. "And I must be equally crazy to let you threaten me and get away with it!" He yanked her close against his naked chest, wrapping his arms around her and capturing her lips in an abrupt assault that contained masculine annoyance, frustration, and a will to dominate.

But no genuine violence.

Selena stood passively still for a long moment, letting the feel of his mouth and hands communicate directly to her inner emotions. And under that impact she knew for certain that he would never really hurt her. The small sigh of relief slipped between her lips and he caught it in his throat as his tongue surged hungrily through the small gate of her teeth.

"Selena, you idiotic female, what in hell do you think you're doing?" he asked throatily against her mouth. "I could tear you to pieces, don't you realize that?"

She buried her face against the warm skin of his chest, instinctively inhaling the exciting, slightly musky scent of him. "You won't," she whispered. "You won't do that, York."

"Where do you get the courage to challenge me like this?" he asked, half in awe as he lifted aside the sweep of her hair and found the nape of her neck just inside the collar of her shirt. "You must want something from me very badly," he concluded strangely.

"I do."

"Don't you know I'll give you anything you want?" he muttered. "I told you once I could afford to keep you in reasonable style."

"You know damn well I don't care about your money. You tried to bribe me once before, remember?" Selena's wine-colored nails bit deeply into the tanned skin of his chest in small punishment.

He groaned, his hands slipping down her back to her hips and arching her intimately against him. "I don't know what you expect me to do. A man doesn't change his ways under pressure. Not a real man."

"I'm hoping a man, a *real* man, can learn to restructure some of his priorities under a little pressure," she murmured.

A ripple of pure male irritation went through him as he held her tightly and nipped the lobe of her ear a bit harder than could have qualified as a caress. "Tell me again that you want me," he commanded deeply.

"I . . . I want you, York. That's why I'm taking the risk," she said simply.

"The risk of getting savaged by me?"

"Deep down I was sure you wouldn't really hurt me." Selena lifted her face and met his narrowed look with the first stirrings of confidence.

He moved his head in a wryly negative way. "Then you had more faith in my nature than I would have had under the circumstances! My God! If someone had told me I'd let myself be blackmailed like this, I'd have told him he was out of his mind!"

"York . . . ?"

"I think there's been enough talking for now," he growled, lifting her back into his arms. "At the moment I need some reassurance!" He started back toward the bed but this time Selena didn't struggle.

"Reassurance that I need you? Want you? York, there's no question about that." She smiled gently up at him but there was no answering curve of his mouth. Instead he seemed to be studying her intently as he set her back down on the bed. "Believe me, York, this will all be for the best. . . ."

"Hush, Selena. I don't want to hear any more about your ridiculous plans. Not tonight. Don't push your luck!"

He stepped out of the jeans and the snug Jockey shorts that did little to conceal the evidence of his rising desire. Selena watched him with a touch of nervousness as to his present mood, but no real fear. She was aware of the beginnings of her body's reaction to the sight of his lean, smoothly muscled frame.

When York came down beside her on the bed, she risked another tiny, hopeful smile. Again there was no response. He reached out to begin unfastening the buttons of her shirt with precise, steady fingers.

"York, it will be all right, I promise you," she tried hesitantly, still uncertain about his mood. There was a sort of calculated deliberation about his movements. It wasn't that he continued to menace her, Selena thought uneasily, but there was something. . . .

"No more words, Selena," he ordered quietly. "I'm going to try another kind of communication with you tonight." He found the last button, undid it, and then slipped his warm palm inside the opening of the shirt to flatten his hand against the skin of her stomach. Selena sucked in her breath and raised her eyes to his in silent inquiry.

This time when she met his unyielding, flaring expression she knew what it was that hung in the air between them. York was grimly intent on gaining her surrender in bed as recompense for his surrender in business. She sensed his need to bind her to him on this most primitive of levels, to exercise the force of his will on her in bed. He would dominate her here in retaliation for her domination of him in the other matter.

He shifted his weight until he was lying heavily across her chest, crushing the soft roundness of her breasts. His mouth came down on hers in hot, aggressive seduction as he unsnapped the fastening of her jeans and pushed the denim down over her hips.

Selena moaned beneath the provocation of his mouth, her reactions to him stirring far more rapidly to life than she would have believed possible. Unconsciously her knees flexed and she lifted her hips off the bed so that he could more easily dispense with the jeans. In another moment they were lying nearly naked, the only scrap of clothing left being Selena's unbuttoned shirt. Lightly she stroked the firm skin of his stomach and thigh, thrilled with the quickly aroused response of his body.

"You're suddenly very eager to please, sweetheart," he mocked huskily, grazing her breasts with his lips and tongue. "Do you think that if you pacify me in bed I'll be more amenable to my fate?"

"I'm not trying to...to..." She broke off, shocked at the implication of his statement.

"You're not trying to bribe me with your body?" he concluded for her.

"No! York, how can you say such a thing?"

"It's all right," he assured her thickly, his hand approaching the contour of her hip and kneading passionately. "Unlike you, I'm highly susceptible to the right form of bribery!"

"You're trying to make me angry, aren't you?" she breathed in sudden comprehension, eyes very wide.

"Maybe it would be better if we both shut up," he groaned, silencing her with his mouth.

And maybe he was right, Selena thought vaguely as she felt herself slip under his spell. Maybe this wasn't the proper time for words. She had run enough risks this evening. With compelling urgency she raked her fingers across his shoulders and into the depths of his hair, twisting her hands through it luxuriously as he explored the honeyed territory behind her lips.

Teasingly at first and then more aggressively, his tongue scorched her sensitive mouth. When she tried to meet the bold caress with a similar one, he seized the opportunity for combat.

Selena, who had never intended a duel, merely a tantalizing response to his tongue, found herself swamped by the assertive force of him. She tried to retreat as he drove into her mouth, tried to pull her head aside only to find her chin captured and held.

The excitement he was generating was undeniable but she had the feeling she was being ravished, seduced, physically dominated. She shouldn't let him get away with this approach, she realized vaguely. But she was at a loss to know how to stop it. Her body was too quick to betray her. Comfortably complaisant in the knowledge that the threat in him was sensual, not violent, she responded wildly under his arousing touch.

Her little throaty gasps of air ended more often than not in tiny, too-revealing moans. York drank them in and then reluctantly tore his mouth away from hers in order to pursue the line of her cheek to her ear. Selena shuddered as he swept the tip of his tongue in a circle and then scraped his teeth across her earlobe.

When she arched her head back over his hand, eyes tightly closed against the rising excitement, York murmured her name hoarsely and moved his palm audaciously to the inside of her thighs.

"You're a handful of fire," he whispered huskily. "I can't wait to see the painting that results from fire!"

He lowered his head to coax the tight nubs of her nipples into throbbing peaks of desire. The fingers feathering the inside of her leg began to move in sensuous patterns that prowled and provoked until Selena was a trembling, pleading creature of loving passion. Gone was any thought of trying to put the sexual battle on an equal footing. She could think only of response and the necessity of completing the union.

"York, York, please," she whispered beguilingly, seeking the firm thrust of him with her gentle hands. He caught his breath as her fingers closed over him.

"Please, what, Selena?" he provoked, trailing damp flames across her stomach with his lips.

"Please make love to me! I want you so much," she cried out breathlessly.

"Show me," he growled. "Go on, my reckless little blackmailer, show me how much you really want me!"

As if the command were a sensual goad, Selena reacted with a burst of passionate aggression that would have stunned her if she'd been thinking rationally. With a half-stifled little cry of desire she flung herself against him, feeling him roll over onto his back as she did so. Selena wound up in a silken sprawl across him.

"Ah . . . !" York's long sigh came from deep in his chest as he twined his fingers into the dark chestnut tangle of her hair. Selena rained hot little kisses across the expanse of his chest, and he used the leverage of his hold on her head to force her lower until her tongue was dipping into his navel.

Selena knew now that she was engaged in a battle with him, but for the life of her she could not have explained or even said whether she wanted to win or lose. The only imperative was to build the seductive tension between them until they were both out of their minds with it.

Her fingers danced along his thigh and up the inside of his leg. There she used her nails in a soft scoring that brought another groan from him.

"My God!"

Entranced with the manner in which he was succumbing to the trap he himself had set, Selena did everything in her power to pursue and arouse. When she nipped a little savagely at the inside of his thigh, she felt the shudder go through him and delighted in it.

The situation had been subtly reversed, she thought in panting excitement. He had ordered her to make love to him, to show him how much she wanted him, and in the process had fallen victim. He was the one who lay helpless beneath the onslaught of passion!

An exultant, purely feminine power seemed to light a fire in her veins. She was now the one in control and she could make this man shiver with his need of her! She flowed along the length of his body, now clenching her fingers into the muscular male buttock, now teasing the thrusting evidence of his desire. Deliberately she tangled her legs in his, wrapping her arms around him as she lay along the full length of him. She was inching her way up his chest, stringing kisses as she went. Soon ... soon she would take him completely, she thought in shimmering excitement. He would learn the full extent of her power!

"I've unleashed a whirlwind," York gritted in wonderment. He stroked back her hair as she advanced up his chest.

"Yes," she agreed, heady with her adventure. And to think there had been a small moment when she had feared this man! Now she had him in the palm of her hand. Briefly she raised her head to look at him, her eyes aglow with the knowledge of her own power and the passion of the moment.

When he saw the look in her eyes, something flickered in York's expression. The green flames of his own gaze leaped higher as he sensed the challenge she was intent on delivering.

"Oh, no, you don't, witch," he muttered thickly. "I didn't start this just to let you take over completely!"

"No! Wait!" Selena protested futilely as she felt him gather himself. But it was useless. With a surge he had reversed the situation once again, swinging her down onto her back and covering her with the full force of his body. Selena's eyes opened very wide for an instant, the breath nearly going out of her as he sank down on top of her slender form. Then she was gasping for air for another reason.

Parting her thighs boldly with his hair-roughened legs, York drove into her softness with all the aggression of the born conqueror. In the space of an instant Selena was made to know the extent of her own surrender.

"York!"

Her arms came around him tightly as she hungrily accepted the fullness of him. "Oh, York!"

For a timeless interval he didn't move within her, content to let her adjust to him and relearn the feel of her secret, pulsing warmth. When he heard his name on her lips and felt her arch upward pleadingly, he began to establish the rhythm that would take them to the outer limits of human pleasure.

But it was a rhythm he set and maintained. No amount of twisting, clinging, or beseeching on her part could persuade him to alter the sensuous pattern. In this he would be master.

Time and again he brought her to the edge of the erotic abyss and time and again York backed off temporarily, half withdrawing from her just as she would have leaped over the edge.

The tantalizing frustration began to be more than Selena could bear. With each trip to the edge she became more and more desperate for the ultimate fulfillment that only he could provide.

"York, please. I can't stand this!" she moaned, urging him with her nails.

When the begging failed, she dug her nails in deeper and swore at him. "Damn you, finish it! I'm going crazy!"

If he felt the fierce scoring of her nails on his back, he gave no sign. But the passion he had loosed in her was affecting even his own iron-willed control. York's purpose may have been to master her with seduction, but he could no longer resist the forces he had set in motion.

With a groan he came to her one last time. Selena wound her legs tightly around his waist in an effort to hold him close but there was no need to trap him. She sensed his control dissolving, leaving him abruptly as much in her power as she was in his.

Together they rode the final surging rhythm and together they found the bursting, sparkling culmination. Their names were on each other's lips as they hurtled into the void, so tightly bound that they were as one being during the final shimmering moments. . . .

It was a long while later before Selena eventually stirred, coming out of the aftermath of their lovemaking with slow laziness. She lifted heavy lashes to find York staring down at her, propped beside her on one elbow. When she questioned him mutely with her soft, loving gaze, his mouth curved indulgently.

"What's the matter, sweetheart? You look quite lost." He brushed his mouth lightly against hers. "Very soft and vulnerable."

"Only because I've just been manhandled by a jaguar," she managed to retort with a tiny, flickering smile.

"Manhandled by a jaguar? That may be a contradiction in terms." York lifted a strand of her hair and settled it behind her ear. There was a sleek satisfaction radiating from his perspiration-damp body. It should have alarmed her but it didn't.

"I don't care." She stretched languidly, finding her ankle still caught between his legs.

He watched her satisfied lethargy for a moment and then smiled in affectionate amusement. "I think we just proved something to each other."

"Did we?" Selena slanted him a glance.

"Something we've known all along. We really can't resist one another, can we?"

"I'd hate to have to try," she admitted, cuddling closer contentedly.

Then she felt the jaguar's claws. "Knowing that, honey, and knowing what we have together..." He nuzzled her gently. "There's no need to let my business interfere in our love affair, is there? We only have to concern ourselves with each other. Call off your blackmail threats, sweetheart. There's no need for them."

Selena froze, emerging abruptly from the blissful effects of his lovemaking. Slowly she turned her head on the pillow to look at him.

"Did you think," she whispered carefully, "that you could seduce me into forgetting all about what you're planning to do to Richard's firm? The answer is no, York. For both our sakes, the blackmail stands. I'm not letting you out of the cage until you learn that there are more important things in life than crushing your opponents!"

The indulgent amusement in him faded immediately and the hard edge of his mouth became almost ruthless.

"You really mean it, don't you? You think you can change me with your puny threats! Damn it, woman, I just had you giving yourself completely to me. Don't you understand that? Pure female surrender!" he clarified bluntly in case there was any chance at all that she had misunderstood the significance of what had just transpired. "You were soft and wild and I'm the one who made you that way!"

Selena heard the sheer outrage in his voice and for the first time she sensed no fear singing along her nerves. She was learning more about her caged cat by the minute. He wouldn't inflict any real damage on her, she told herself anxiously. Not now. If there had been a risk of that, it was earlier in the confrontation.

Still wary, but no longer fearful, she glared at him. "Putty in your hands, York? I've got news for you, demonstrating your abilities in bed doesn't automatically mean you can dominate a woman outside of it!"

"A little something else you're going to teach me while you're reshaping my world view?" he mocked tersely.

"Why not?" she dared.

He stared at her as if he couldn't quite believe what he was hearing. Then with a short, thoroughly outraged oath, he swung his feet off the bed and reached for his clothes.

"You've got nerve, lady, I'll say that for you," he snapped as he flung on the jeans and shirt. "I only wonder if you realize what a fine line you're walking! You're not going to get away with it, you know,'' he added as he located his shoes. ''You won't be able to go on making your blackmail threats by day and giving yourself to me by night. You haven't got enough nerve for those tactics. You want to play dangerous games with me? Okay, we'll play games. And when it's all over and you've lost, I'm going to take a lot of satisfaction in listening to you admit I've won! More satisfaction,'' he claimed as he headed for the door, ''than I'm going to take out of destroying your ex-boyfriend!''

Selena lay very still in her bed and winced as he slammed the door behind him. She had challenged the jungle beast in his lair and she would have only herself to blame if she lost the battle.

Eight

Selena's decision to slip into Nola Eden's art class was a spontaneous one made over a breakfast of coffee and a croissant. She sat alone at a tiny table in a sidewalk café on South Lake Avenue, reflecting moodily on the fact that she was going to have to continue her search for the perfect croissant in Pasadena. The one in hand lacked that indefinable flaky, buttery quality. And along with that thought came the memory that Nola was scheduled to give a class at Artistic Endeavors that morning.

It was exactly what she needed, Selena told herself resolutely. Anything to take her mind off the hopeless tangle in which she'd involved herself. She would simply tell the staff at Artistic Endeavors that she'd returned early from the skiing holiday but didn't intend to come back to work just yet. With a nod to herself in recognition of the brilliant solution of how to spend her morning, Selena paid her bill and hurried back to her apartment to collect some supplies.

Forty-five minutes later she was applying great sweeps of orange and purple acrylic paints onto a canvas under the direction of an instructor who was every bit as colorful as the art being created.

"Forget the shape of the teapot!" Nola Eden cried dramatically as she paced up and down the aisle of students in the skylit room behind the sales floor of Artistic Endeavors. Her flowing, jewel-toned caftan wafted around her grand and stately figure, and her silvering black hair was drawn into a regal bun at the back of her handsome head. Nola loved giving these classes. "Forget the shape of the teapot. Any fool with a little high school shop art can draw a teapot. We are not photographers! We are not trying to reproduce literally what anyone can see with his own eyes. We are looking for something beyond what the average viewer sees. We are trying to get down on the canvas an aspect of that teapot that is totally unique!"

Selena bent obediently to the task, frowning intently as she sought to free her mind in order to see the still-life arrangement in front of her in a new light. What was York doing this morning? Had he gone straight home from her bed last night? Was he plotting? Against her? Against Richard?

"Damn!" Furious with her inability to shut out thoughts of the jaguar who was hunting her, Selena took a disgusted swipe at the canvas instead of the carefully planned brush stroke she'd intended to make. Seeing the result, she ruefully chewed on her lower lip. The painting assuming shape in front of her was a chaos of color and design. Talk about venting one's frustrations!

"There is a lot of energy in that," Nola Eden pronounced, coming up unexpectedly behind her, "but it is out of control this morning, Selena. You must control the painting, not let it control you!"

"I'm afraid my concentration is a little weak today," Selena confessed.

Nola peered at her. "You are too easily distracted, Selena," she opined with sudden, almost gentle understanding.

Selena looked at her, mouth twisting wryly. "That's always been the problem, Nola, you know that. It isn't just this morning."

"Art doesn't have to be the be-all and the end-all for everyone who tries it."

"It does if one wants to make a success out of it." Selena shrugged, touching up a spot on the edge of the canvas. She stared at the little stroke of color she'd just added, aware of Nola eyeing it equally critically.

"But for you it will always be a hobby, won't it, Selena?"

"I'm afraid so. Did you always know you were going to be an artist, Nola?"

"Since I picked up my first crayon." The older woman smiled reminiscently. Then she moved her head in a little negative gesture. "But you, I think, will come and go from art all your life. It will always be important to you..."

"But not the most important thing," Selena concluded quietly, eyes still on her painting.

Nola considered that for a moment. "You know as well as I do that you have some talent. If you worked at it, developed it..."

"But I won't. I know that by now. I shall be content for it to remain a hobby. There are too many other things in life, Nola. Too many other things that I like as much as I like art."

"People? The business side of art?" Nola hazarded curiously.

"And...other things."

"Ah, a man."

Selena lifted startled eyes to study her instructor. "How did you know?"

One stately shoulder lifted in an almost Gallic shrug, a mannerism Nola had picked up while studying for a year in France. She didn't bother to answer the question directly.

"If..." Selena paused to reflect on her own words before continuing. "If I were meant to be an artist, I would be able to turn the intensity of my feelings into my work. As it is, they merely serve to distract me from it instead."

"Because he is more important to you than your art."

"Yes. And I'm a very selfish woman, Nola. I want to be more important to him than his work."

"For you that's not selfish. That's a necessity," Nola stated with great understanding.

"Is it wrong to want to change someone, Nola?" Selena fixed her friend with a look of honest anxiety.

"The question is irrelevant," Nola retorted with grand authority. "It can't be done." Then, seeing the flash of pain in Selena's eyes, she smiled gently. "I don't believe a person can be changed in a fundamental sense, but he or she can be guided into new paths, if those paths promise something more important than the original ones did."

"If the original path is ultimately destructive . . . ?" Selena began earnestly.

"The one doing the changing must see that for himself, Selena. You can only show him an alternative."

"And for some people the alternative would never be as compelling as the original goal."

"It depends on what sort of compulsion is driving an individual, I think." Nola smiled.

What, fundamentally, was driving York Sutherland? Selena wondered. If the need to win was as basic to his personality as Nola's commitment to her art, there was probably no chance of persuading him into a different path. But if his approach to life was a survival characteristic that had served him well until now but was no longer needed, perhaps there was a possibility . . .

Sudden prickles of awareness flashed through her system as Nola moved off to another student. Only one man could ruffle her thoughts without even interrupting them verbally, and Selena turned with a sense of resignation to find York letting himself quietly into the classroom. His searching gaze found her at once across the aisle of students and half-finished canvases.

Selena forced down the instinct to hide, disgusted with herself. She stood clutching a paintbrush in one hand, watching York's dark figure as he paced toward her with the intensity of the hunt. His charcoal gray pinstripe suit was a swath of darkness amid the casual, vivid attire of the students.

"Hiding out again, Selena?" he murmured far too blandly as he came to a halt, looking over her shoulder at the orange-and-purple teapot she had been painting. He studied it with great interest. "Let me give you a tip. When you're trying to stay undercover, never use a familiar locale. Makes it too easy to find you."

"Not enough challenge?" Selena managed to retort, her eyes following his as they rested on the canvas. It was much easier than looking at him. Every nerve had come alive the moment he had walked through the classroom door. Memories of last night put all else out of her mind. She must never forget that York Sutherland was now after surrender. It was the only way he knew how to attack a problem.

"It was easy enough to find you this time," he drawled, turning his head to smile dangerously at her.

"That's because I wasn't trying to hide. Why do you always have to think in hunting terms?"

she hissed angrily. "I merely chose to attend an art class being given by a friend."

"You knew I'd be calling you this morning. You haven't been in your apartment since seven-thirty," he said starkly.

"I'm on vacation! And how was I supposed to know you'd be calling? You left in something of a huff last night, as I recall. You were muttering a lot of macho threats as you went out the door, not promises to call first thing in the morning. How *did* you find me, anyway?"

"I called the store as soon as it opened to see if you'd checked in. One of the clerks knew you had dropped in on the class. What's going on here, Selena?" he added with apparent interest as he examined the room from behind the lenses of his glasses. "The sign said free classes."

She slanted him a glance. "Artistic Endeavors sponsors the classes, but believe me, they're worth it in the long run!"

"Students become so inspired that they race out and buy up half the supplies in the store?" he guessed with a quick, knowing grin.

"It's a business," she muttered, turning back to her painting.

"Your idea?"

"The free classes? Yes."

"Sounds like a good marketing technique," he allowed. "I can see how it might be very effective."

"Thank you. Coming from one who knows business as well as you do, that's praise indeed!" she said with determined lightness.

"You seem to know a lot about business yourself," he said with deceptive mildness. "At least, you've certainly been set on proving your knowledge lately."

The red stained Selena's cheeks but she refused to rise to the bait.

"What is this supposed to be?" York went on inquiringly. "Don't tell me you're doing that teapot over there!"

"I'm doing an *aspect* of that teapot," she ground out, striving to keep her voice low. "There's no point simply trying to reproduce a camera-image of a teapot. Anyone can do that!"

"I couldn't," he surprised her by admitting.

She blinked uncertainly. "Well, with a little training in sketching, I'm sure you could. Come to think of it, you must have had some drawing practice somewhere in your career as an engineer. Here! Do something!"

She thrust the paintbrush into his hand before he realized what she was about.

"Selena, I didn't come here to paint teapots..." he began in abrupt annoyance.

"I know. But see what happens, anyway," she chuckled, suddenly intrigued by her own idea. Hastily she set up a new, inexpensive canvas board on the easel. "Go ahead. Put something down on all that white surface," she urged, hazel eyes gleaming.

He eyed her narrowly and then looked at the canvas with deep suspicion. "I wouldn't know where to begin."

"The first thing to do," came the unexpected voice of Nola Eden behind them, "is to forget about all the details of the teapot and find one single aspect of it that you want to convey."

York tossed an assessing glance over his shoulder at the stranger. Selena made introductions quickly. "Nola, this is York Sutherland. York, this is our instructor this morning, a very fine artist herself. Nola Eden. Listen to her. She can not only do art, she can teach it. A rare combination."

Nola smiled encouragingly. "Let's see what you find most interesting in the shape of that teapot, Mr. Sutherland."

There was a short contest of wills before York astonished Selena by turning back to the canvas and sinking his brush into a blob of yellow acrylic on the palette. When he moved, it was without any hesitation at all, producing a sweeping curve of color on the white surface. Nola and Selena stood silently as he added another richly textured brush stroke. Then he dipped the brush into a vibrant red brown and swooped down once more on the painting.

The shapes emerging on the canvas would have been hard to identify as a teapot, but there was a full, rich, rounded feel to every line. Selena stared first in puzzlement and then in growing embarrassment as the utter sensuality of the curving strokes dawned on her. She flicked a sidelong glance at Nola's intent face and then looked away quickly. Perhaps it was all her imagination. She was so aware of every little nuance of emotion when she was around this man. Perhaps she was overreacting . . . ?

There was silence around the canvas several moments later as York tossed down the brush and swung around to pin Selena. "Satisfied?" he demanded sardonically.

She licked her bottom lip anxiously, trying to think of a response. It was Nola who came to her rescue. The older woman studied the yellows and reds of the indefinable teapot and said slowly, "It's obvious you've had no formal training, Mr. Sutherland."

"Not even in kindergarten," he agreed with an inclination of his head.

"But there is a tremendous amount of energy and a sense of strong emotion in those brush strokes. You have literally assaulted the canvas, but what you've produced is not dark or angry as I would have expected. It's rather sensual, in fact." Nola lifted her head and beckoned the other students imperiously. "Come here and take a look at this. What do you think?"

Already curious about the obviously out-of-place stranger in their midst, the other painters gathered about York's rendition of a teapot.

"He's definitely caught the full curve of the bottom part of the pot," remarked a slender, long-haired young man as he stood wiping his brush on a cloth.

"And I like the stark clarity of the colors. I spend so much time mixing my shades that I think I forget how effective the full intensity of the hues can be. Dazzles the eyes, doesn't it?" added a young housewife who always came to the classes offered by Artistic Endeavors.

"Interesting treatment of the handle of the pot," nodded another intelligently. "You feel you could put your hand on that particular shape of yellow. It has a nice full feeling to it."

"But not heavy or overblown," Nola inter- jected. "There's a delicacy about the strokes that is hard to describe. A very interesting teapot, Mr. Sutherland," she concluded with a brisk nod. "Very interesting, indeed."

York arched one black brow, casting another glance at his handiwork. "Especially when you take into consideration the fact that I wasn't try- ing to paint the teapot at all," he said calmly. "That, Ms. Eden, is a picture of a woman I went to bed with last night. Or rather," he added pre- cisely as he caught Selena's horrified expression, "it's an impression of the way she felt in my arms. Marvelous sense of anonymity in modern art, isn't there? The rest of you mistook her for a teapot."

How she managed to put away her materials and escape from the smiling, speculative glances of her fellow classmates, Selena never knew. York waited for her patiently, fully aware that he'd won the latest skirmish.

So thankful was she to escape from Artistic Endeavors, Selena didn't even protest when York put a firm hand under her arm and led her out- side to a waiting gunmetal gray Mercedes.

"How could you?" she finally got out tightly. She sat stiffly in the leather seat, her yellow T-shirt and paint-stained jeans a contrast to the elegance of the car. The chestnut hair, which she had tied back in a short ponytail, had started to come loose and tendrils dangled haphazardly around her neck. In the artistic environment of the painting class, she had been almost stylishly at home. Here in the understated luxury of the Mercedes, with York sitting beside her in his pinstripe suit, Selena felt ridiculous. "How could you do that to me, York?" She stared straight ahead, her gaze unseeing as he piloted the car through the noonday traffic.

"You told me to paint a picture and I painted a picture," he retorted calmly.

"You were supposed to be painting a teapot, for God's sake!"

"Why would I waste my time painting a teapot? I could care less about that damn teapot! You were the only thing on my mind when you pushed that paintbrush into my hand!" he growled.

Selena snapped her head around to glare at him. Then she saw the spot of yellow on the charcoal gray suit. All at once she felt a good deal better. She might be feeling ridiculous dressed as she was in York's car, but yellow acrylic paint on a charcoal gray pinstripe was even more incongruous.

"You did it to punish me, didn't you?" she charged. "You told Nola and the class that it was a picture of me as a way of getting even with me for having forced you to try painting!"

"I told them the truth. I wasn't trying to punish you. As a matter of fact, I found the whole thing a rather interesting experience."

"I'll bet!"

"What lesson were you trying to teach me, Selena?" he asked, his voice suddenly softening as he slanted a glance across the seat at her.

She closed her eyes for an instant. "I don't know," she finally sighed. "It was an impulse. I just had this crazy idea of forcing you to do something that couldn't be seen in terms of winning or losing. But you managed to turn it all around on me, didn't you? You made me the loser."

"That's not true, honey," he protested quietly as he turned the Mercedes into the drive of a fashionable row of townhouses. "I wasn't thinking in terms of punishing you or of winning or losing. I just did what came naturally to me when you forced me into that particular situation."

"And what comes naturally to you is winning. Please, let's get off the subject," Selena added in low appeal. "Where are we?"

"My place. I've brought you home for lunch."

"But, I hadn't planned on . . . I mean I . . ."

He was out of the car and opening her side of the vehicle before Selena could formulate the protest. Warily she climbed out of the leather seat and glanced around. It was one of Pasadena's recently renovated neighborhoods, not unlike her own, but definitely more expensive. There was no "old money" feel to the area, as there was on the side of town where Richard Anderson lived; rather, one sensed that the people who lived here were up-and-coming, aggressively successful. It fit York well.

In spite of her frustration and bad temper, Selena felt an undeniable curiosity about the sleek, modern environment in which York lived. She could hardly complain about the modernness of the place, she told herself silently as she took in the patina of real leather upholstery and polished wood floors. Her own home, after all, would have to be described as distinctly modern. But whereas her sophisticated apartment was full of the unique and the amusing, York's home was rather formal in style. Very masculine but somehow aloof. Once over the shock of her eclectic collection, people tended to relax very quickly in Selena's home. It would take a while to unwind here, she thought. A man like York should have a more suitable place for relaxing, not a home that reminded one of the lobby of a fine hotel.

"I intend to impress you with my talent at the barbecue," York was saying as he removed his jacket. Selena saw his wry frown as he caught sight of the yellow paint on the lapel but he manfully said nothing about it.

"I'm not very hungry, York."

"You'd better be. The steaks have been marinating in teriyaki sauce since this morning. Wait here while I change," he ordered, disappearing up the staircase.

"I'm surprised you were in a mood to think of feeding me this morning," she couldn't resist taunting as he vanished temporarily from sight.

"It's this theory I'm developing about how to handle blackmailers," he called down from the bedroom. "When sex doesn't work, try food."

"And if that doesn't work?"

He came to the top of the staircase and grinned down at her, strong hands braced on the railing. A devil looked out of his eyes. "I'll think of something. I always do."

"More unsubtle threats, York?" Selena took in his jeans and open-throated shirt. Apparently he had no intention of returning to the office that afternoon. Her eyes never left him as he came easily down the staircase.

"Just a little something for you to worry about when you have nothing else to do," he told her enigmatically as he reached the bottom and turned to lead the way into his kitchen.

"Psychological warfare," she muttered, following him slowly. "But it won't work, York. On this one issue you won't win. I really will carry out my blackmail plans if you go through with your attempt at revenge."

He shot her an examining look as he pulled a glass dish containing two luscious steaks half-buried in teriyaki marinade out of the refrigerator. "Why are you so determined to change me, Selena?" he asked with quiet urgency. "What's wrong with the way I handle my life? Do you think I would have gotten where I am today if I didn't know how to win?"

"Probably not," she admitted honestly. "But are you sure it's wise to go on using the same approach? Maybe it's been necessary to be hard and ruthless up to a certain point—"

"Damn necessary," he interrupted feelingly as he directed her outside to a private walled patio that contained the barbecue grill, an outdoor table and chairs, and several hanging plants. Beyond the wrought-iron gate Selena could see a glistening pool that was undoubtedly shared by the townhouse homeowners. "I started out with nothing, Selena," York was saying bluntly as he built the barbecue fire. "My parents were killed when I was sixteen years old and they hadn't had much, so there was nothing left to leave me."

Selena sank into one of the patio chairs, poured herself a glass of chilled white wine, and listened with a sensation of something between sympathy and amusement. Sympathy because she believed every word York was saying and amusement because she knew exactly what he was trying to do.

"I learned very early that a man has to set goals for himself and let nothing get in the way. I worked nights and went to school days. When I graduated from college, I figured out exactly where I wanted to go with my career and took advantage of every opportunity that came along..."

"And made a few for yourself when they didn't come along on schedule?" she guessed dryly.

"There's been nothing illegal about what I've done," he grated, prodding the steaks with a long fork. He looked up and met her eyes. "I haven't always played with kid gloves on but I've never played unfairly. That's saying something when you consider the side of town I came from."

"What side was that, York?"

"The wrong side, honey. Believe me." He reached for a small carving knife and tossed it lightly into the air. Selena stifled a gasp of dismay as he deftly caught it by the handle and then threw it with a movement that was faster than her eye could follow. The blade cartwheeled wickedly in the air and came to rest, point down in the redwood table beside her, handle quivering.

"Very impressive," she managed gamely. "A little something you picked up on the streets over there on the wrong side of the tracks?"

"I'm afraid so," he murmured, turning back to the steaks.

"I can see why you're not overly nervous of blackmailers."

"Oh, hell, Selena. I wasn't physically threatening you and you know it!"

"No?" She poured disbelief into her voice although she hadn't, in truth, really thought he was trying to frighten her. "Just attempting to make a small . . . point?"

He reached for his glass of wine and took a long sip. "Just trying to illustrate the fact that there is a rough side to me and it isn't going to change. It may not be very pleasant, but it's served me well. I want you to accept that and then forget about it because it won't have anything to do with you and me."

She ignored that last statement, having argued fruitlessly about it too many times already. "York, you don't need those knife-throwing skills any longer. Literally or figuratively. You're off the streets now. Maybe it did take a certain ruthlessness and a vendetta mentality to get you out of the jungle, but if you continue to use those techniques in civilization they'll only become self-destructive. You can't separate your life into compartments and say that in one you'll be vicious and in another you'll be sophisticated and in still another you'll be kind. Everything's interrelated!"

"There speaks the artistic side of your nature," he told her indulgently.

"Oh, for heaven's sake! Why do I even try?" Selena asked bitterly, knowing the answer even as she asked the question. She was in love with the man. It was probably the nature of a woman in love to attempt the impossible because deep down she didn't really want to accept that it was impossible!

To her astonishment, however, York was taking the rhetorical question seriously. "You try, I think," he said with a slow nod, "because you're a little afraid of me. You're not sure I can contain the harder side of my nature, so you've decided it would be safer if I were to abandon it altogether.''

"You don't understand.'' She stared down at her wine.

"Yes, I think I do. You're the one who doesn't understand, Selena,'' he returned quite gently. "Part of your fear, I'd be willing to bet, is that you don't have any way of knowing whether or not I value my victories for any length of time.'' He trapped her startled glance and smiled beguilingly. "But you don't have to worry on that score. One thing about having come up the hard way—I have learned to appreciate everything I've earned. I take care of my possessions, sweetheart. I'll take care of you. I won't grow tired of you as if you were a toy with no real value. I don't go after toys with this much effort, believe me!'' he concluded very steadily.

In the taut silence that followed his words, Selena sought for a suitable response and nearly failed. Had that been one of her fears? "Are you trying to tell me that your family motto could have been, 'What I have, I hold'?'' she got out with forced lightness.

He arched one black brow behind his glasses. "It could have been. If I'd had a family that went back more than one generation. We didn't worry overmuch about ancestral mottoes where I came from.''

Selena tried to shake herself free of the spell he was weaving. But before she could say anything else, he was adding quietly, ''Selena, I want you. You must know that by now.''

''But what do you want *from* me, York?'' she asked tonelessly. ''I've never been quite sure of that part. I'm not a breathtaking beauty. I'm not from the highest rung of the social ladder. I've lowered myself to the level of a blackmailer. What can you possibly see in me?''

''I could ask you the same question,'' he pointed out softly. ''But neither of us could ever ignore the other, regardless of how and where and when we had come together. I think you know that.'' His mouth twisted with sudden wryness. ''Just ask yourself why you're working so damn hard at the thankless task of behavior modification!''

''While you're asking yourself why you're submitting to blackmail?'' she dared.

''Don't remind me,'' he groaned, accepting her attempt to lighten the charged atmosphere. ''Bring the plates over here, woman. I want you to taste the artistic heights to which I can take a mere steak!''

But he paused in the act of transferring the juicy aromatic meat to her plate and met her eyes very directly. "I could have given you a more complete answer to your question, sweetheart."

Selena waited, aware of a breathless feeling.

"I could have tried to explain to you that, perhaps because of my background and the way I go through life, I have a need for your warm passion and your caring. I want your intelligence and spirit and gentleness. I need your laughter and your sympathy and your integrity. Do you understand?"

The breath Selena had been holding seemed permanently blocked in her throat. The gray-green gaze that held her so tightly was a bond against which it was useless to struggle. Bravely she gathered the total force of her willpower in an effort to avoid succumbing completely.

"What makes this relationship so complicated, York, is that those are exactly the qualities *I* need and want in a man."

Nine

The startled anger that came to life in his face was enough to break the spell. With more courage than she would have given herself credit for, Selena turned back toward the redwood table and began to help herself lavishly to the salad that had been brought out earlier. She was shaking and she was terribly afraid it might show as she picked up the tongs.

"Don't think I'm not properly appreciative of all attempts to appeal to the softer side of my nature, York. I'm aware of what you're trying to do by giving me your life history. You want me to feel a womanly need to comfort the strong, tough, macho type who has had to face the rough side of life head-on. But I'm not going to play the role of the sweet, devoted little woman who turns a blind eye to the harsher edges of her man.''

"So you're going to try and blunt those edges?" he snapped, spinning her around to face him just as she set down her plate. The green depths of his eyes were glittering with a variety of emotions from impatience to challenge.

"Yes!" she stormed tersely. "I am! In spite of that lovely catalog of my virtues that you just finished reeling off, the fact remains that I'm not all sweetness and light, York. I may have had a comfortable middle-class upbringing and I may lack your driving ambition in business, but I'm not completely soft! I know what I want in life and I'm capable of—'' Selena broke off, horrified at where the reckless words were leading her.

"And you're capable of resorting to blackmail to get it?" he finished ruthlessly, although there was a hint of satisfaction and amusement in his eyes now. "I suppose I should be flattered, shouldn't I? You let Anderson go without even a backward glance, but I'm getting the full reform treatment.''

"Don't you dare laugh at me, York Sutherland!"

"I'm not laughing at you! I'm torn between the satisfaction of knowing you want me as badly as I want you and the frustration of having you willfully toss out this stupid red herring." He pulled her closer, fingers digging into her bare arm below the sleeve of her T-shirt. "One of us," he stated grimly, "is going to have to give."

"Last night you said I would be the one who surrendered," she flung back, sparks flashing in her eyes at the memory.

"Oh, in the long run I'll still make good on that threat," he said easily. "But for the moment you win."

Selena stared, astonished at the simple words as York sat down at the table and began to tackle his steak and salad. "What did you say?" she got out incredulously.

He glanced up and then went back to his steak. "You heard me."

She sat down shakily, ignoring her own plate. "Just like that? You'll give me your word not to pursue your plans for Anderson & Company?"

"Well, there is a small condition attached," he allowed thoughtfully.

"Which is?" she demanded furiously.

"That you move in with me. Share the same bed with me, the same breakfast cereal, the same newspaper and electricity bills," he spelled out firmly, pinning her with an unrelenting expression. "I want you to come and live with me, Selena."

Trying to catch her breath and her thoughts, Selena found herself unable to look away from his intent, aggressive expression. "When did you..." The words wouldn't come the first time around so she tried again. "When did you make this decision?"

"I've intended all along to have you living under my roof," he returned with an arrogance that made her long to kick him.

"I meant," she gritted, "when did you decide to give in to... to my blackmail threats?"

"Oh, that decision." He shrugged carelessly. "I made up my mind about that while I was in the process of painting the picture of you in Nola Eden's class. How soon can you move in?"

"York! I can't!" Selena faced him, stricken with the enormity of what it would mean.

"You mean you won't?" he clarified, calmly cutting another slice of steak.

"I mean I can't. It's...it's too soon. There are too many problems to be worked out between us and... and ..." Selena tried to calm her runaway thoughts as she recovered from the effects of the two grenades York had just thrown at her. "And you know perfectly well I would be taking a tremendous risk. You'd use the intimacy of a situation like that to wear down my defenses and you know it!''

"Probably," he agreed unrepentantly as he reached for his glass of wine.

"I knew it!"

"No man wants his woman to have any defenses against him. He wants to know she's really his, on every level."

Selena shook her head, a little panicked. "But in this case you'd have a very specific goal in mind, wouldn't you? You'd be deliberately trying to get me to forget about my blackmail threats so you could go after Anderson & Company."

He considered that and then asked quietly, "Do you particularly relish the idea of our relationship being based on a balance of power? That's what you've set up, you know. You're forcing us into the roles of adversaries. You've armed yourself with threats of blackmail, and all I've got on my side is the knowledge that we want each other very badly. Do you blame me for trying to use my weapon after having been bludgeoned by yours?"

She stared at him helplessly. "I didn't know how else to force you to change, York. Blackmailing you was the only thing I could think of at the time.''

"Okay, I accept that you had your reasons even if they were crazy. You've won. I'm going to leave Anderson to some other fate than the one I had devised. Now I'm countering your move with one of my own. In return for my agreement to abandon my plans for Anderson, I want something in exchange. I want you to come and live with me.''

Selena swallowed, thoroughly alarmed at the quagmire that was suddenly yawning at her feet. "York, we can't go on like this!''

That brought a slight lift to the corner of his mouth. "Now that has a familiar ring to it.''

"I'm serious! *This* is serious!''

"I'm aware of that,'' he retorted dryly.

"What you're proposing is an endless series of skirmishes. You surrender to my blackmail threats only to turn around and make a counter-demand. If I give in to that, you'll use the advantage you've gained to control me and force me to stay out of your business affairs. I'll be put in the position of trying to find another lever to use against you. It could go on and on until we wind up destroying each other.''

"You started it,'' he murmured bluntly.

"And you're trying to finish it by making me realize how hopeless it all is," Selena concluded wrathfully, leaping to her feet. "But it's not going to work! I'm not accepting your counter-move, do you understand? The blackmail threat, as you choose to term it, stays the way it is."

He leaned back in his chair in that lazy, menacing sprawl, eyeing her coolly. The fingers of one large hand tapped idly on the redwood tabletop as he appraised her taut figure. "You can't win, sweetheart. Pack it in and call it quits," he finally advised. "You're going to wind up living with me sooner or later and you know it. Come to me now and it will be a fair exchange of power—my promise to leave Anderson alone for your promise to move in with me."

"But that's just it," she shot back huskily, bracing herself against the chair. "It won't be a fair exchange of power. You know very well that once I'm living with you I wouldn't be able to . . . to . . ."

"You wouldn't be able to go on blackmailing me? I'll admit I would like to break you of that habit before it becomes fixed," he drawled. "And yes, I think if I had you living here with me it would be fairly easy to convince you that such tactics were unnecessary. You're not cut out for this kind of warfare, honey. And as far as I'm concerned, while I can handle it in my business life, I'd just as soon not have it invade my personal life.''

It was tempting, Selena thought unhappily, so tempting to just give in and stop fighting him.

What was he doing to her? What had he already done, for that matter? She found herself still frantically trying to sort out her thoughts while she lay alone in her own bed that night. It should all have been simple and straightforward. One fought fire with fire. But she was quickly learning that there was a flaw in the old adage, a flaw that York himself had pointed out to her. How could she go on with a relationship in which each party was always conscious of having a lever to use against the other?

York had claimed he would abandon his plans for Richard's company. To all outward appearances she had at least managed to deflect him from one of his goals. That should have been a victory of sorts. York Sutherland had actually been made to choose between two goals and he'd chosen her...while painting a picture of her that was supposed to have been a teapot!

Selena gritted her teeth. But of course it hadn't worked out that simply. Irresistible forces weren't stopped that easily, as she was coming to learn the hard way. He wanted her to come and live with him, did he? He knew she couldn't keep up the skirmishing in the intimacy of a mock marriage!

A mock marriage. The words made her catch her breath as she lay staring blindly at the ceiling. Even if all the other problems were cleared away, would she really want to live with York Sutherland on his terms?

With a shock of acceptance, Selena knew that what she wanted from York was marriage, a real marriage.

One more complication in an already complex tangle, she thought sadly. How long could she maintain the fragile balance of power? He was such a skilled campaigner. Look at the way he'd played his hand this afternoon. There had been no attempt to persuade her into bed this evening. He had simply taken her home after the scene at lunch and left her politely on her doorstep, every six-foot-plus inch of him radiating masculine power and assurance. He knew how to handle her, his manner said more clearly than words. What made her think she could hold out against him? He wanted her and ultimately he would have her on his terms.

Selena swallowed anxiously at the thought. She had known from the beginning the man was dangerous. Who would have guessed just how dangerous?

Tormented throughout a sleepless night by devastating images of capitulation to York and the possible consequences of not surrendering, Selena fell into an uneasy sleep shortly before dawn, only to be awakened around ten o'clock by the ringing of the telephone.

Sleepily she fumbled for the receiver, not realizing who would probably be on the other end until it was too late.

"It's mine, babe," were York's first words, and even through her sleep-fogged brain the repressed jubilation in his voice came through to Selena. She sat up in bed, frowning bewilderedly.

"What's yours?"

"The contract," he explained in tones of great satisfaction. "The one Sutherland, Inc., was bidding for along with Anderson & Company. I got word this morning that a decision was made late yesterday afternoon. Sutherland, Inc., walked away with it, hands down!"

Selena caught the immense wave of pleasure, relief, and quiet celebration flowing toward her over the phone line and responded to it unthinkingly.

"York, that's great! Congratulations! We'll have to celebrate," she said spontaneously.

There was a brief pause. "Yes, we'll celebrate my two latest acquisitions," he replied with the arrogance of victory. "A new contract for my firm and a mistress for my home. I'll pick up a bottle of champagne this afternoon and come on over to your place. How does that sound? I can get away from here early..."

"York, that's not quite what I meant," Selena interrupted firmly. "You know I haven't agreed to live with you. I need more time—time to think it all through. And on second thought, I'll be able to do that more clearly if you're not around. Could I take a raincheck on that celebration?"

The controlled frustration in his tone was evident. "I suppose I can afford to give you another twenty-four hours," he said grudgingly. "But beyond that I won't make any promises. You're mine, sweetheart, and sooner or later you're going to have to come to terms with that fact!"

The receiver went dead in Selena's hand and she sat staring at it, slightly stunned by his confident certainty. It was only as she finally replaced the phone in its cradle that the full implications of York's early-morning wake-up call came home to her.

With the settling of the contract bidding, she only had one arrow left for her bow. She could no longer threaten to leak the bid figures if he went ahead with his plans to destroy Anderson & Company. For the first time Selena realized the precariousness of her remaining threat to warn Richard of the takeover plans.

What if York were carrying on his manipulations without letting her know that he planned to go through with them? How would she know until it was too late? She only had his word, Selena thought, that he was submitting to her blackmail threat.

Her teeth sank painfully into her lower lip as she swung her feet out of bed and headed for a shower. No, York would fight her fair and square. That was the way he fought his battles, she was certain of it. He wouldn't sneak around behind her back, accomplish his goal, and then throw the victory in her face. That wouldn't be the kind of victory he'd want.

Was there something to be said for being wanted that ruthlessly? Selena asked herself suddenly just as she was in the process of inserting her left contact lens. The thought shook her so much that she dropped the little circle of plastic and had to scramble about on her knees for a few minutes before locating it under the sink.

But the thought persisted. York wanted Anderson & Company but he seemed to want her with an equal passion. He could be proceeding with his plans for Richard's company without her knowledge, but Selena's intuition told her he wouldn't take that route. Which meant he wasn't prepared to risk losing her by circumventing her puny attempts at blackmail. He'd go on fighting her over the threat, naturally. That was predictable given the nature of the beast. But the battle was an honorable one. He wanted to make her back down first before he continued his war on Anderson.

An honorable opponent.

Selena told herself she mustn't risk romanticizing a situation that was not at all romantic, merely very, very dangerous. With a grimace she turned away from the mirror and finished dressing. She had a lot of thinking to do in the next twenty-four hours. She only hoped that would be time enough to come up with the right answer.

Ten

Selena was up, dressed, and packing by six-thirty the next morning. Wearing the stained and faded denims she used for painting and an emerald green pullover, she padded barefoot around her apartment in a driven, intense mood that would have done credit to a great artist or a great businessman.

She knew what she had to do. There was no point dragging out the painful skirmishing any longer. Sleep had refused to come, even in the last hours before dawn as the decision had slowly crystalized. Once it had been made, Selena knew it was the only answer left.

Right or wrong, painful or risky, she was going to move in with York.

If the offer was still open.

That last thought made her mouth twist wryly as she carefully folded newspaper around a delicate mobile of polished crystal. Perhaps after all her hesitating York would be having second thoughts himself about his decision!

Then Selena's hazel eyes hardened determinedly. Too late. She was on her way and York would just have to make room! She hadn't tried to fool herself in the wee hours of the night. She hadn't wrought any miracles in the traumatic days since she had taken up York's challenge. He was still the same man she had labeled as dangerous the first time she met him.

But she did know a great deal more about him, Selena consoled herself. He had his own strict brand of integrity, he could be tender and, considering that she had been trying to blackmail him, remarkably patient. Even as she lifted a painting of what appeared to be a crazed unicorn off her kitchen wall, however, Selena knew she was banking everything on one other aspect of his nature. She was praying he had meant it when he'd told her he valued his victories.

By seven thirty most of the artwork had been packed, leaving the white rooms looking somewhat forlorn and bare. Selena decided she deserved a cup of coffee. It was going to be a long day. She sat sipping the coffee and staring at the telephone, wondering exactly when and how she was going to notify York of her decision. Perhaps, she decided with a sigh, it would be easiest to simply let him find her sitting on his front step, waiting for him after work!

And if he laughed at her capitulation she would never recover.

By eight-thirty she was ready to take the first load of boxes down to her car in the underground garage. It was going to take several trips to get even the essentials over to York's townhouse. As tempting as it was to take the easy way and let him find her waiting on the front step tonight, it made a great deal more sense to take the first load over early this morning and get the keys from him so that she could continue moving during the day. Selena glanced at the clock. He would probably be leaving for work soon. She had better hurry.

The wired energy on which she had been running in lieu of a good night's sleep was propelling her rapidly toward her goal now. She scooped up several small boxes full of art objects and stacked them so high in her arms that she couldn't see over the top. She groped blindly for the doorknob and managed to get the door open.

"What the hell . . . !"

York's fierce growl of surprise as she collided with him made Selena gasp in dismay.

"York! What are you doing here?" she yelped as the boxes tumbled from her hands and scattered on the carpet. She lifted startled, agonized eyes to find him staring at her with a look she couldn't initially decipher.

"Running away again, Selena?" he finally asked almost wearily, shoving aside a box with his toe and stepping into the room. "Are you really so afraid of me?"

Automatically Selena stepped back as he advanced into the living room. His gaze swept the denuded walls and end tables, took in the pile of waiting boxes, and finally came back to her. This time Selena realized she understood that look in his eyes. It was pain, the rawness of which was becoming more obvious by the second.

"I'm not running away, York." The words were amazingly steady considering her jangled nerves. But the necessity of soothing that pain in his eyes was paramount. Soothing this man's pain would always be the most important thing in her life, Selena realized in a flash of insight.

"Your twenty-four yours are up," he said, his jaw tightening as he shoved his hands into the front pockets of his dark slacks and spread his feet slightly in an aggressive stance. "Did you really think I'd let you run away without a confrontation?"

In spite of her decision to surrender completely to this man, Selena still felt her hackles rise at the challenge in him. Her chin lifted.

"Do I hear the beginning of a threat? Poor York. The only thing you know how to do is fight, isn't it?"

To her astonishment the ebony lashes lowered briefly in an expression that could have been despair. When they lifted again, there was a shimmer in the gray-green gaze that Selena knew with sudden agony could only be moisture.

"Dear God, Selena," he whispered starkly. "Please don't go. Please don't run away from me, I couldn't..."

"York, no!" Selena reacted at once to the desperate, tortured rasp of his words and the promise of tears in his eyes. She launched herself at his chest, her palm coming up to cover his mouth as the gathering tears in her own eyes spilled to her cheeks. "Hush, my darling, don't say such things. Don't ever say such things. I wasn't running away from you—I'm running *to* you. You big idiot, don't you know when you've won? I'm the one doing the surrendering, so please don't cry and beg me not to go. It ruins everything!"

His arms came around her so tightly that she could scarcely breathe. "Selena," he murmured huskily into the depths of her hair. "What are you saying? Are you really coming to me? Are you moving in with me?"

"Yes, oh, yes, York. If you'll have me..."

"No," he grated roughly. "No, not on those terms. I couldn't bear for you to be the one who surrenders. Don't you understand? That's the reason I came here this morning! To tell you that I'm finished with the skirmishing. All I want is you, sweetheart. I don't give a damn about Anderson's firm. I knew when I came back from Utah that if I were forced to give up the takeover plans because of you, I'd do it. That's why I spent the extra day up there. I had to think. Never in my life had I made business decisions based on pleasing another human being."

"I don't want you to make your business decisions on that basis," she said almost violently. "I never meant to tell you how to run—" She broke off, because of course she had tried to tell him exactly how to run his business, and his life. How could she deny it? "I shouldn't have threatened you," she went on humbly. "It was just that I was so desperate for you to set new priorities. I wanted to be more important to you than your revenge against Richard. I wanted you to see that revenge was destructive and instead I almost wound up destroying us!"

"You were always more important to me, sweetheart." His hand moved soothingly in her hair as he pressed her face more deeply into his shoulder. "I just didn't understand why I couldn't have both. When you said you didn't want me to have both and were prepared to resort to blackmail over the matter, I dropped the revenge thing. There was no question about my priorities. You soon filled all my thoughts, anyway. I began to lose interest in wreaking vengeance on Anderson the moment I made you mine."

"But you didn't tell me because it went against your nature to let me think I'd won so easily?" she hazarded, sniffling a little as a smile of pure happiness touched her lips.

He groaned. "I wanted to teach you that trying to manipulate me wasn't the answer. I didn't want a relationship based on a series of power plays. On the other hand, I've grown so accustomed to being the one in charge and having everything on my own terms, I honestly didn't know how to just say, 'I quit, you're the win-ner.' At least," he added with great depth of feeling, "I didn't know how until a few minutes ago when I thought you were running away from me again!"

She drew back her head, looking up at him through lashes that still sparkled with tears. "You're too late, darling. I quit first. You're the winner." Selena lifted her palm to his cheek and he turned his mouth into it lovingly.

"No, the victory is yours. I couldn't stand for you not to have it. All I want is you, not another win." The green in his eyes was warmed with an emerald fire.

"Are we going to stand here and battle over which one of us gets to do the surrendering?" Selena whispered throatily, her heart in her eyes. Her mouth curved tremulously. "I am, after all, the one who was packing to move in with you this morning..."

"And I'm the one who showed up on your doorstep first thing to tell you that you could have anything you wanted, including control of Sutherland, Inc., if you would marry me!" he countered softly. "I love you, Selena."

"Marry you! Oh, York, yes, please. I would like to marry you more than anything else on this earth. I love you so much!"

The remainder of her confession of love was lost against his mouth as he hauled her urgently close and claimed her lips. The kiss was everything that made up the two of them—strength and gentleness, passion and love, even some of York's natural aggression and Selena's spirited fieriness. But they all blended together in a harmonious whole that would never be separated.

"My darling, my love," York finally whispered, lifting his mouth reluctantly to gaze down into her glowing face. He shook his head as if in wonder as he touched the corner of her mouth with his thumb. "Why have we wasted all this time trying to outmaneuver each other? Some things are so much better than winning...."

"And some things have nothing at all to do with losing," she concluded gently.

"But if we're intent on this mutual surrender," York began deeply, "there is a place for it. A very suitable place." He saw the answering response in her warm and loving expression and bent to lift her into his arms. "And there couldn't possibly be a better time. My sweet love, I have been hungering for you all night!"

Selena touched the side of his face as he carried her toward the bedroom. "You mean to tell me you didn't sleep well last night, either?"

"I didn't sleep at all!" He walked into her room and over to the still-unmade bed. "Over and over again I kept telling myself I had to find a way to stop the confrontations before you gave up on your task of changing me and told me to go to hell!"

"I'm told a person can't be fundamentally changed," Selena said quietly as he stood her on her feet beside the bed.

"He can learn to recognize different priorities, though," York growled, spearing his fingers through her hair. "Didn't you see how quickly I made you my number-one priority? There was certainly enough evidence around!"

She looked up at him, glorying in the feel of his hands in her hair. "What do you mean?"

"Do you think I normally chase after women who try to humiliate me by running off constantly?"

"I never ran off! I simply chose to go my own way on a couple of occasions! I certainly wasn't trying to humiliate you."

"And do you think I routinely let women blackmail me?" he pursued, his mouth touched with love and wry humor.

"Well, I suppose not, but there wasn't much you could do about it, was there? I had the leverage to get away with it because I'd seen those figures in Utah."

He shook his head slightly at her naiveté. "There was no way you could have followed my plans at work. I could have tied the whole thing up into a package, hit Anderson & Company with it, and you wouldn't have found out until it was all over."

"Ah, but I knew you would never do a thing like that." It was Selena's turn to smile at his naiveté. "You may be ruthless at times, but I knew you'd fight fair."

He arched a mocking brow at that, removing his glasses with a sigh of resignation. "I don't know what made you think I'd feel any obligation to play fair with a blackmailer."

"Intuition," she told him succinctly, her fingers going to the knot of his striped tie.

"That," he drawled as she slid the tie from around his neck, "must have been the little voice I kept hearing that assured me you wouldn't be resorting to threats unless I meant something to you! I took heart from that, you know."

"Interesting. I didn't know men had intuition." Selena opened the first button of his crisp white shirt and slid her fingers enticingly under his collar. She watched him with flaring eyes.

He started to bend toward her, his own hands gliding over her hips and up under the light material of the emerald pullover she wore. Then he stopped. "Then there was the painting I did of you." He grinned a little wickedly. "Now that was one hell of a clue about how I felt. Didn't you have any idea of the level to which you had reduced me when you stuck that paintbrush in my hand and forced me to do a picture?"

"Not at the time," she admitted. "What *did* it mean to you?"

"When I'd finished it and I realized that somehow it really did convey the impression of what it's like to hold you in my arms, I was as surprised as you were. That's the point at which I realized I had to find a way of getting us out of the battle zone."

"Your method, as I recall, was to try and convince me to compromise!"

"I should have had the sense to get down on my hands and knees right then and there and call the whole thing off," he muttered, burying his lips against her throat as his hands moved along the warmth of her stomach up to her unconfined breasts. "I'm learning, sweet Selena. Give me a chance. I'm capable of change. For you I'd do anything!"

She heard the conviction in his voice and sagged heavily against him. "I don't want to change you, York. I only want to know you're mine. I just want to know I'm as important to you as you are to me."

"I intend to spend the rest of my life proving exactly how important you are to me," he rasped huskily, lifting his mouth from the curve of her shoulder long enough to remove the pullover completely. "Accept my surrender, sweetheart."

"If you'll accept mine." Selena wrapped her arms around his neck, nestling close. The texture of his shirt rubbed against her breasts as his hands kneaded sensually down the length of her slender back.

His heated gaze flowed across the invitingly parted lips and down to where her nipples thrust against his shirt. "I accept," he said with roughening passion. One hand still moving probingly at the base of her spine, York undid the rest of his own buttons until the shirtfront fell open. Deliberately he pulled Selena close and she felt the tremor in him when her breasts were finally crushed against the tangle of hair on his chest.

Selena's soft moan seemed to inflame him. With a swift movement that belied the fine shaking in his fingers, York unbuttoned the fastening of her jeans, found the zipper, and shoved his palms down the curve of her hips.

As the jeans were peeled away from her body, he went down on one knee before her, worshipping her with damp, hungry kisses that brought her breasts to an aching fullness and then made her draw in her stomach with a tremulous sigh of passion.

Selena's hands locked in the thick darkness of his hair as his tongue came out to flick the sensitive skin at the contour of waist and thigh.

"York, oh, York . . ."

When his teeth nipped in sensual aggression, she thought she would collapse. The flames he was stoking in her began to burn. As if sensing her uncertain balance, York eased her to a sitting position on the bed, slipping off the jeans entirely. Kneeling in front of her, he caught her wrists tenderly and the lambent fire in his eyes was a barely controlled inferno.

"I knew I wanted you from the first time I saw you," he told her huskily. "I won't deny that in the beginning part of that desire was tangled up with a need to take you away from Anderson. I thought it all fit very neatly into my plans. I could have you and also have one more victory over the man I intended to destroy. But you must believe me, Selena, I realized almost immediately that there was a shift in my motives. I wanted to take you away from Anderson but not because I wanted to use you against him. I just couldn't stand the thought of you in his arms! It drove me out of my mind thinking of him holding you, kissing you..."

Selena lifted her chained wrists to frame his taut features between gentle palms. She smiled lovingly, understandingly. "I love you, York," she told him simply. "I never loved Richard."

His fingers tightened on the small bones of her wrists and there was a half pleading, half challenging flare of emotion in the green gaze. "You were afraid of me..."

She shook her head, mouth curved beguilingly. "Definitely *wary,* but not afraid. In any event, it wouldn't have mattered. I was also very fascinated by you. I told myself that if you weren't quite so dangerous I would let myself fall head-over-heels for you. In the end I did anyway, even knowing you were as dangerous as I had thought! In my mind you were an irresistible force..."

"That you wanted to control by being an immovable object?" he hazarded ruefully.

"A little," she confessed softly. "No, a lot. Were you very angry with me, York, when I took it into my head to blackmail you?"

His mouth twisted a little dangerously, a little devilishly. "I wasn't exactly pleased but, as I mentioned earlier, I consoled myself with the thought that you wouldn't be trying such tactics unless you really cared about me. If there hadn't been that element in your motives, you wouldn't have used blackmail to change me, you would have gone straight to Anderson and told him everything."

Selena looked at him with helpless longing, loving the morning scent of him as it reached her nostrils. It was filled with the essence of his maleness, overlaid with the freshness of the shower he'd probably taken less than an hour ago.

For a moment longer their eyes held and then, wordlessly, York turned his lips into the palm that cradled one side of his face. The delicately erotic kiss he placed there made Selena draw in her breath and half-curl her nails against his cheek.

Slowly he moved his mouth to the inside of each of the wrists he still held, kissing the vulnerable area lingeringly. Selena shivered and he must have felt it. When he released her hands it was to part her legs with a sensual inevitability that she had no wish to resist. Kneeling there in front of her, he bent his head to kiss the inside of her thighs.

"Oh, my God, York," she murmured. "Love me, please, please love me."

He eased her back onto the bed with a hoarse groan of desire, coming down along the length of her but not yet completing the union. Urgently Selena wrapped him close, arching herself into him and finding the line of his throat with her mouth. She loved this man, and knowing he loved her made her world complete. She could give him everything because he was willing to give her the same.

With excruciating tenderness York explored every inch of her body. His fingers probed delicately, enticingly, and his tongue curled first around each nipple and then went to the pulse point at her throat. Selena twisted with gathering passion, soft moans coming more and more rapidly deep in her throat.

"I love the feel of you coming alive in my arms," he rasped. "I only want you to love me and go on loving me forever!"

"Forever," she echoed throatily, her senses spinning round and round as they threatened to slip out of control. "Oh, York...!"

As the intensity of her need communicated itself to him, York's tender, enticing lovemaking changed, becoming more passionately aggressive. It suited Selena entirely. She writhed luxuriously in response, her nails biting deep into the resilient male buttock and then finding the contour of his shoulders.

When she felt she could stand no more of the teasing, provoking forays he was making, he suddenly slipped his thigh roughly between her legs, making a space for himself near the heart of her warmth.

"Now, Selena, I must have you now!"

He was pressing against her, testing her softness with a surging power that thrilled every fiber of her being. With slow, heart-stopping deliberation York entered her completely.

For a long moment they held each other in utter stillness, acknowledging the sense of oneness and the pulsing vitality of their love on its most fundamental level. Selena clung to the rockhardness of this man who filled her senses, delighting in the feeling of surrender that was also victory.

"York, my darling, my love . . ."

Unable to resist the pull of her words and the passionate hold that enveloped him, York began to move, establishing the cadence of their lovemaking with a primitive force that swept all before it.

Selena didn't try to fight the swirling mystery that awaited her. Joyously she gave herself up to the delight and the passion of York's arms. The taut, twisting tension within her was quickly stretched to the point of explosion, and when the convulsive shiver of completion shook her, York growled her name in a kind of triumph, his face buried in her hair.

Selena cried his name into the void, urging him to join her, but even as the tides of her own release began to recede she was aware of the fact that he still resisted the final satisfaction.

Tingling, violently aware of him still filling her body, Selena looked up at him with lazy contentment, her lashes veiling her gaze seductively.

"Oh, York..." she breathed on a sigh of pleasure, her fingers lifting to trail through his hair. "I feel as if I've been swept out to sea."

"It isn't time to go back to shore yet," he gritted as the last of her tremors died away. She heard the tautness of heavy passion in him and opened her eyes wider, questioning him silently.

Her answer was the reestablishment of the rhythm that had just brought her to fulfillment.

"Oh!"

Her already sensitized body reacted as if to a torch. The heat and power of him scorched this time, wringing an incredible response from every inch of her. Selena couldn't even control her own breathing.

"Selena! My God, Selena!" There was no attempt on York's part to prolong the ecstasy of their mutual passion this time. She knew from the abandoned, reckless way he lost himself in her that he couldn't have resisted even if he had wanted to. She knew the excitement of female triumph even as he took his own, very masculine victory. Holding each other as if they were the only two beings left in the universe, Selena and York hurled themselves headlong into the fireworks of their mutual satisfaction.

It was a long time later that Selena finally found the strength to stir against the warm hardness of York's sprawling, contented body. His arm tightened warningly around her but he didn't bother to open his eyes.

"Where do you think you're going?" he inquired lazily.

She grinned, waiting for him to lift his lashes and meet her gaze. When he finally did so, the green depths held a lifetime of loving promise.

"I know this isn't terribly romantic, but the honest truth of the matter is that I've got to go and rinse off these contacts of mine. Tears and contact lenses don't mix. I feel as if I've got sandpaper in my eyes!''

He chuckled deeply, moving a hand down the length of her body to pat her curving bottom with possessive affection. "It's all right, you know, I would have fallen for you even if you didn't wear contacts and even if you'd never had the advantages of braces.''

"A likely story!''

"It's true," he told her firmly as she scrambled off the bed and hurried to the bathroom, where she quickly removed the lenses and rinsed them off. "How could it have been otherwise? We were made for each other.''

Selena popped the contacts back in and came to stand in the bathroom doorway, surveying him with laughter and love. "I didn't realize you were such a romantic!''

"It's not a question of romance, it's a matter of practical physics," York lectured sternly. "Don't you know what happens when the irresistible force meets the immovable object?''

"An explosion?''

"That's the popular misconception," he scoffed. "The truth of the matter is that they combine their powers and together become totally invincible." He held open his arms. "Come

back to bed, my sweet Selena, and I'll demonstrate."

Selena went back to bed.

* * * * *